THE
Tin Man

THE
Tin Man

A Novel by

Robert W. Graper

Rev. date: 07/19/2021

To order additional copies of this book, contact:
Xlibris
844-714-8691
www.Xlibris.com
Orders@Xlibris.com
832000

CONTENTS

This book is dedicated to two fellow authors:

Dale MacMillan
Dwight V. Murray

both of whom were instrumental in encouraging
me to write and publish this book.

CHARACTERS

(in order of introduction)

Bob Garver – (main character) instrument engineer who moved from the Massey Chemical plant in Belle Park, Ohio, to the Deer Park, Texas, olefins plant start-up team.

Doc Harpy – instrument technician working for Controls, Inc.

"Long John" Whippet – instrument technician working for Controls, Inc.

Frank Baron – Bob Garver's boss and leader of the Massey Deer Park olefins plant start-up team.

Bob Esterbrook – electrical engineer at the Massey Belle Park–Ohio plant; he suggested that Bob Garver consider hiring on with Massey.

Fred Conway – former instrument engineer at the Massey Belle Park–Ohio plant; he was moved to the Massey Houston office. Bob Garver was hired to replace him at Belle Park. Fred would later be one of three start-up team coordinators for the olefins plant start-up.

Ralph Swenson – when in sales, Bob Garver used to call on Ralph at the Massey Chemical plant in Wood Creek, New Jersey, when he worked out of the Philadelphia office of Moore Products Co. He became Bob's boss at Massey head office Engineering.

Mark Langston – engineering manager at the Belle Park Plant; Bob Garver's boss when hired at Belle Park.

Jack Fishbane – one of three start-up team coordinators for the olefins plant start-up. He would later be promoted to be leader of the start-up team in addition to his coordinator role.

Bud Asperson – operations manager over the high pressure boiler area; Fred Conway's nemesis.

Harold Neymeir – instrument engineer on the olefins start-up team. He spoke with a German accent and had transferred from an overseas company to work at Massey.

Mike Bourne – Massey operator who was killed in an explosion.

Betty Marcum – police lieutenant working for the Deer Park Police Department; headed the arson investigation.

Mike Sanchez – police sergeant working for the Deer Park Police Department.

John Cross – electrical engineer on the olefins start-up team.

Simon Wemple – forensic sketch artist working for the Deer Park Police Department.

Cindy Parker – Betty Marcum's apartment roommate.

Major "Moose" Miller – Bob Garver's superior officer while in the army.

Jack Lentor – FBI agent; former boyfriend of Betty Marcum.

Joe Lighten – police sergeant working for the Deer Park Police Department.

Randy Michaels – Massey Deer Park plant safety manager

Lou Samuels – Massey Deer Park plant manager

Marcus Stalinbeck – the Tin Man; the arsonist who caused all the Deer Park plant fires and explosions.

Mark Simmons – an instrument engineer at head office (minor character).

John Swisher – vice president of operations at the Massey Chemical Company.

Lou Docker – manager of head office Engineering

Penny Lusher – the hit man (woman) who attacked in the Shrimp Galore restaurant.

Lyle Talbot – utilities process engineer; involved in the plant instrument air hot cutover.

Rich Michaels – the separation section operations manager; involved in the plant low-temperature shutdown.

John and Marsha Marcum – Betty Marcum's parents.

Bill Marcum – Betty Marcum's brother.

Bill and Linda Garver – Bob Garver's parents.

Mack Turner – Deer Park police officer who was a computer hacker (Mack the Hack).

Sam Peck – Deer Park police officer; hacker working for Mack Turner.
Don Lancy – pastor of Faith Community Church.
Linda Marker – wedding coordinator
Mary Lenox – soprano to sing at wedding.
Randy Simcon – FBI camera expert
"Bull Dog" Sumner – John Swisher's lawyer.

CHAPTER 1

BAPTISM OF FIRE

It was a long way from Ohio. When Bob Garver accepted the move to Houston that the Massey Chemical Company offered him, he never expected to be standing in the pouring rain at 4:00 a.m. watching two instrument technicians working on a valve while standing on the top of a scaffold twelve feet off the ground. It followed Bob's first day on the olefins plant start-up team. His new boss, Frank Baron, had told him to get this valve repaired at all costs, if it took all night. The valve was keeping the demineralizer from running, and the boilers could not run without demineralized water. Otherwise, minerals would plate out on the boiler tubes, making production of the 1,200 PSIG steam inefficient and causing early failure. This high-pressure boiler steam was used directly in the two big fifty-thousand-horsepower steam-driven process gas compressors. The high-pressure steam was also reduced in pressure in several "let-down" stations for many other lower-pressure uses in the complex. No steam from the boilers meant the whole complex was down cold. So Bob Garver, the "newcomer," was put on the graveyard shift to "git 'er done," like Larry the Cable Guy says. Bob was being tested since he was the new kid on the block.

The start-up team had been assembled with instrumentation, analyzer, and application engineers mostly from the Houston area. The boss was trying to see what this northern Yankee could do. Bob was thirty-two years old, stood slightly over six feet tall, weighed 180 pounds, and was in pretty good condition. In Ohio, he had been a regular at the Muscle Builder's Gym, and he played quite a bit of golf. But here, in the Deer Park, Texas, plant, he was looking up into the driving rain, trying to see what the two instrument technicians were up to. His physical condition wasn't helping him here.

He yelled up to them, *"Have you got the valve out of the line yet?"*

They did not answer his question. In fact, he thought he heard one of them mumble some words better not repeated.

The rain increased, and lightning began to flash across the sky as though all of the Fourth of July fireworks had gone off together. A chemical plant like this one, with its tall metal distillation towers, seemed to attract lightning hits. It became apparent that the instrument technicians were questioning the sanity of working during this downpour and, more importantly, questioning the sanity of the instrument engineer down below observing the work.

As Bob looked up, a wrench fell off to his left, and he heard, *"Whoops!"*

Then two large flange nuts came down on his right, and another voice from above said, *"Look out below!"*

As Bob often remarked in this sort of situation, *"My momma didn't raise no dummies!"*

So he yelled up to the technicians, *"Come on down, let's get out of the rain, this is crazy!"*

They waited all of thirty milliseconds and climbed—or better worded, *slid* down the scaffolding. The trio ran to the truck and drove to the instrument shop located in the center of the complex.

The rain only seemed to increase, beating on the tin roof of the shop with a deafening roar, like God had called in His percussion section and turned up the volume. These "frog stranglers," as Southerners referred to them, were new to Bob. He had been born and raised in the northeast, where rains were usually gentle. He suggested that they all take off early for lunch and go to the local eatery for pizza—on his dime. Off they went in Bob's old four-wheel drive Jeep. Fortunately, the streets were not yet flooded to the point where they could not make it. Houston, called the Bayou City, is known for street flooding during heavy rains. The bayous are big ditches that form a network that eventually drains water into the Gulf of Mexico miles away. But during heavy rains, the bayous back up because they cannot handle the volume of rain pouring into them. When this happens, it causes the water to back up into the streets. Many a driver has tried to plow through water that looked shallow, only to find out that it was high enough to stall the car. In fact, folks trying to drive through water under highway underpasses have found themselves stranded, wet, standing on top of their cars, awaiting rescue. About the only people who like these heavy rain events are the car repair mechanics. Fortunately, Bob and the instrument crew made it to the Brick Oven Pizza restaurant in Deer Park without incident.

Lunch was a good opportunity for Bob to learn a bit about the two technicians. They did not work directly for Massey Chemical—they worked for Controls, Inc., an instrument maintenance contractor. Doc Harpy, a short, stocky, 5'4" guy came across as tough as nails. "Long John" Whippet was about 6'10" tall, thus explaining his nickname. Bob would later learn that both of them were excellent at their jobs. During lunch, Long John told a story about how Doc Harpy reported to work wearing a women's Maxi-Pad the same day he had been operated on for hemorrhoids. During the shift he had to climb up and down several ladders to work on instruments. Ouch!

Doc just laughed and said, *"Ya gotta make a livin', don't ya?"*

Long John had played basketball while in Pasadena High School. He still held the record for the most points scored in one game, and was obviously very proud of it. Talk about records—on this night, both men showed themselves fully able to consume a complete eighteen-inch pizza each. Bob was no slouch in the area of eating, but chose to take some home for later.

Bob used the time to brief the men on some of his background to make them more comfortable with this "stranger"—and worse yet, this "Yankee." After graduation with a BS in chemical engineering, he had spent seven years with Moore Products Company, an instrumentation manufacturer, working in Philadelphia and Pittsburgh as a sales engineer. Since the new Olefins Unit was built using Moore instrumentation, his transfer to the start-up team was a natural fit. Two of these seven years he was released by Moore for a tour of duty as a first lieutenant in the US Army. A year following his move to Pittsburgh, he was promoted to sales office manager, and moved again, this time to South Charleston, West Virginia, to open their new sales office. He was able to increase sales for two years in a row; however, future difficulties loomed on the horizon. His company only manufactured pneumatic instrumentation—but the oil and chemical industry was rapidly beginning to move toward electronics. The customer that gave him the most business was already committed to that direction.

Bob said, *"I could see big trouble ahead for this poor ol' salesman!"*

He was offered a job by one of Moore's competitors for more money than he was making. However, as he considered the position, he remembered that the man he would be replacing had a "miracle year" the year before, where he sold a huge computer system. That would be next to impossible to duplicate. In addition, the new company had a reputation for firing folks if they did not produce sales quotas quickly. He did not take the job.

Bob also told the guys, *"Being in sales always bothered me. I sold instruments to various companies, but I never got to actually see them in use. Fortunately, I was offered a job with Massey Chemical, at the plant I called on in Bell Park, Ohio. And that's the long story about how I hired on to Massey."*

As he often did in sales, he had taken the Massey Bell Park acting instrument engineer, Bob Esterbrook, to lunch. Esterbrook was actually the plant electrical engineer, but he was temporarily substituting for Fred Conway, an instrument engineer who had been moved to Houston. Massey Chemical was looking for a replacement for Fred—the sooner the better as far as Esterbrook was concerned. During lunch, Bob related some of the "downside" of sales engineering, just to make conversation. Esterbrook suggested that he interview for the position of instrument engineer at the Bell Park plant. Bob agreed and met the personnel manager and engineering manager after lunch.

One of the customers he had called on while in Philadelphia was Ralph Swenson at Massey's Wood Creek, New Jersey, plant, so he used him as a reference. Ralph was later to become Bob's boss at head office, in Houston.

Bob summed up his story to the two technicians by saying, *"Anyhow—I quit Moore and went to work for Massey."*

He explained to the technicians that after three years at Bell Park, he had now been transferred to the Deer Park olefins plant start-up team. Humorously, Long John and Doc gave him their verbal "condolences." By this time, the instrument technicians were joking and having a great time—after all, the pizza was free! They had recovered from their encounter with Noah's Flood.

By the time they left the pizza joint, the rain had become a drizzle, so they went back to the demineralizer and pulled the valve out of the line, taking it to the instrument shop. After removing the pneumatic operator from the valve body, they found and removed a piece of welding rod wedged in the valve port, which had kept the valve from closing. Apparently, whoever welded the pipe failed to check for trash in the line, and it "accidently" got swept into the valve during start-up. From that point on, the valve was impossible to close. Later events would bring that "accidently" conclusion into question. The valve was reassembled, tested, and reinstalled at the demineralizer. Operations was informed that the work order should be closed. By this time, the midnight shift was drawing to a close, and Bob thanked the two technicians and bid *adieu* to his newfound buddies.

*   *   *

Bob stayed over into the day shift to inform Frank Baron (his new boss) what they had found and that the valve was back in service—mission accomplished.

He played up the lightning-and-rain angle, implying that he was almost electrocuted but that he wanted to *"win one for the Gipper."*

Frank said, *"Yeah, right!"*

The boilers were being supplied with demineralized water, and were coming back on line. Frank was pleased that his "newbie" from Ohio had accomplished the job. There were no parades or ticker tape, but it was obvious that Bob had made the team.

Before quitting for the day, Bob decided to call his old boss, Mark Langston, at the Bell Park plant. Timing was right, since Bell Park was on eastern time and Deer Park was on central time—Mark had been at work for a couple of hours. Bob brought Mark up to date on his move and described his "baptism of rain" the first night. He kidded Mark that the olefins plant was so big that the instrument pneumatic tubing (typically one-fourth-inch diameter) was an eight-inch pipe! He joked that the whole Bell Park plant would fit in one corner of the olefins plant control room! He also reminded Mark that he had been promised a position at Massey's head office after the olefins start-up was complete and that he was looking forward to it. Before ending the call, Mark said he remembered his promise, and wished him all the luck in the world.

The sun was bright, the rain had stopped, and things were looking up.

CHAPTER 2

THE ELECTRICAL FIRE

Frank Baron, instrument start-up team leader and Bob Garver's boss, organized his team into three groups. Fred Conway, who Bob Garver had replaced at the Bell Park plant, was appointed leader over the three (3) high-pressure boiler start-ups. Jack Fishbane was made responsible for the eight (8) pyrolysis furnaces and the gasoline hydrotreater start-ups. And Bob Garver would follow the start-up of the process gas compressors, the refrigeration compressors, the light olefins separations section of the plant, and the butadiene unit.

Since Bob's section of the plant would be the last to start up, he was assigned various troubleshooting tasks. One of the first problems involved the level control on the boiler deaerator vessel. Boilers are temperamental beasts, and they cannot use water with high levels of dissolved oxygen. A deaerator uses steam to heat the water to the full saturation temperature corresponding to the steam pressure in the deaerator and to scrub out and carry away dissolved gases (thus de-air-ating the water). The present problem was that the level on the deaerator continuously cycled up and down around 30 percent of the vessel diameter. Several folks had looked at the problem and tried to "tune" the level controller on the control room panel board. Tuning a controller involves adjusting how much action the controller makes on the process, and how fast it takes that action. All of their attempts at tuning had not improved the level cycling; in fact, it had become worse. So Frank Baron sent Bob out to tune the controller.

On his way to the control room, it was necessary to walk under the main pipe rack. On a plant as big as the olefins plant, this pipe rack was multilevel. The main pipe rack had three (3) levels, carrying so many pipes that it literally blocked the sun. Even at 10:00 a.m., it was almost like late dusk. The darkness during daytime made Bob feel rather eerie as he walked the five hundred yards to the control room; and the strange equipment everywhere he looked had his imagination going wild, making him think he might have wandered into a field of cast-off robots. Quickly, due to some motion on his right, he snapped back to reality.

Entering a motor control center (MCC), he caught a glimpse of a man wearing an aluminum hard hat with a brim that totally encircled the hat. This was rather unusual since aluminum conducts electricity, so wearing an aluminum hat in an electrical MCC is not wise. It attracted his attention because modern plastic hard hats only have a small bill in front, similar to a baseball cap but smaller. The man was limping. It was none of Bob's business, so he continued on to the control room.

After watching the deaerator level cycle a couple of times, and listening to the operator talk about, *"You d*** instrument guys have it all messed up,"* Bob decided to make sure the field instrumentation was working correctly. One of the things he had learned during his time at the Bell Park plant was that you can't solve every problem in the air-conditioned control room. Once in the field, he climbed the ladder on the side of the deaerator to look at the level transmitter. It was a differential pressure transmitter that essentially measured the height of the water in the vessel (and thus the level). Everything looked like it had been properly installed and was working correctly. He then climbed down to look at the control valve that added water to the deaerator when the level was low. By chance, as he walked up to the valve, it moved from fully closed to fully open in about three seconds. This should not happen, so he looked at the valve closer.

Eureka! The valve positioner, a device mounted on the side of the valve operator, is designed to accurately position the valve (thus the name). But on this valve, the valve positioner lever that senses the valve's position had come loose from the valve stem. This meant that it could not sense the position of the valve. It was working its little heart out though. When the controller sensed the level was a bit too high, it told the valve positioner to move the valve closed a small amount to reduce the water flow into the vessel. But because the valve positioner lever couldn't "see" the valve position, it continued to drive the valve until it was fully closed. Of course, this lowered the level too fast and too far, causing the valve positioner to attempt to open the valve to compensate. Because the link with the valve was broken, it then drove the valve completely open.

He had found the reason for the level cycling. The broken link caused the valve to be either fully open or fully closed. On the ground below the valve, he found the clip that normally fastened the valve positioner lever to the valve stem. In a few seconds he reinstalled it, and the valve immediately moved to midposition. He waited a few minutes to make sure the valve was making small moves to compensate for changes in level. Back in the control room, the level controller recorder was now drawing a straight line—no cycle. Bob was happy, and the operator had stopped knocking *"those d*** instrument guys."* From scum to hero in one easy step.

Walking back to the start-up trailer, Bob was on top of the world, and couldn't wait to tell Frank Baron that he had solved the problem where others had failed. Once again, in the semidarkness under the main pipe rack, he noticed the man with the aluminum hard hat, this time running away from the MCC. His limp was more noticeable when running. This, too, was unusual since Massey discouraged folks from running in the plant. But Bob's mind was on "bragging rights" to Frank Baron.

So when he arrived, he told Frank, *"The level controller that was cycling is now drawing a straight line."*

Frank Baron stared at Bob, and asked, *"Can you walk on water too?"*

Bob said, *"Yes, but the water has to be frozen."*

Frank said, *"You were the fifth person I sent out there to tune that controller. What controller settings solved the problem?"*

Bob told him the problem was not the controller tuning, but the control valve. He described the problem and the solution.

Then he rubbed it in a little by saying, *"Frank, not all problems can be solved in the comfort of an air-conditioned control room—you have to go to the field once in a while!"*

Frank rubbed his chin and smiled. *"You're right there! I can't believe everyone else missed it!"*

Bob mentioned the man in the aluminum hard hat by the MCC, but Frank didn't think a tin hat, although unusual, was anything to worry about.

He said, *"In the old days, that was the kind of hat everybody wore."*

Frank was in his sixties and had been around the instrument business since Hector was a pup. He kidded Bob that maybe this was the Wizard of Oz's Tin Man on the loose in the olefins plant. Bob laughed, but it wouldn't be long before this unusual person would become a person of interest.

It had been a good, productive day; and since it was still wintertime, dusk was falling, and the lights were on. Everything had essentially settled down into its normal routine. The instrument start-up team was getting used to its accommodations in the start-up trailer, and most importantly, the coffeepot was working. Before leaving work, Bob decided he would make one last check on the deaerator level control, so he headed for the control room. As night fell, the area under the pipe rack was even more eerie than normal although the lights were on. These seemed to accentuate the shadows, and he had to rein in his imagination. He was about halfway to the control room when it seemed like every siren in the entire complex went off at the same time.

Several folks were looking around trying to determine what the problem was. Suddenly, in the direction of the control room where he had been heading, Bob could see sparks falling from the pipe rack down to the ground. It looked like an upside-down fireworks display. He took a second to thank the Lord that he had not been under that section when it started. He would learn later that sparks were also shooting fifty feet in the air, and it was apparent that there was an electrical fire close to the control room. The main pipe rack walkway was dimly lighted at this hour, but the lights suddenly went completely off, leaving it quite dark since night was falling.

In the darkness, Bob noticed sparks, actually melted metal, beginning to fall from the pipe rack above him. A couple of pieces hit his hard hat and fortunately glanced off without burning him. Then, suddenly, it was like the sparks increased tenfold, and it became apparent he was in danger. It was time to use his high school track experience—he violated the Massey rule against running, and did a 440-yard dash in record time back to the start-up trailer.

Within ten minutes, the plant fire engines arrived and attempted to drive down under the main pipe rack to the control room. But the fire was in front of and above them in the pipe rack entering the control room, so they could not get as close as they would have liked. It was obvious from the sparks shooting everywhere that this was an electrical fire, so water could not be used to extinguish the blaze, or it would endanger the firefighters.

One of the plant operators headed for the main power disconnects and shut off power to the entire plant. Now everything in the olefins unit went dark except for the emergency lighting that operated on batteries. With the main power shut off, the source of all the sparks stopped, but the firemen still needed to deal with the fire. Fortunately, one of the fire engines was equipped with an electrically resistive foam, and within thirty minutes, they had the blaze under control. But the damage was done, and it was extensive.

Bob learned later that the plant control room operators had been trying to shut down the plant from the control room, but many of the process controls did not respond, and most of the process status indicators were sitting at the bottom of their scales. This made sense since the wiring and tubing to and from the control room to the field devices ran through the electrical fire area. But a positive going for them was that the instrumentation shutdown systems were designed to be fail-safe. Pneumatic valves were designed to fail to the safe position if and when the tubing was broken or, in this case, burned through.

The shutdown system valves were also designed to shut down on power failure; however, the shutdown systems were equipped with uninterruptable power supply (UPS) systems to prevent unnecessary shutdowns. This was normally a good thing, but in this case, when the power was cut to the entire unit, the UPS systems kept power on for the shutdown systems, keeping some of the shutdown valves in the run mode. As the electrical fire damaged conduits carrying shutdown wiring, current obviously stopped, and several shutdown actions occurred, but in random order. *Fail-safe* sounds great, but when the events happen randomly as they did when tubes and wires are being burned through, things got dicey for a while. Fortunately, the operators were able to bring the plant down safely with no loss of life, although one operator suffered burns from the falling sparks. However, the heart of the plant had been destroyed, and the fire damage was massive.

The electrical wiring and pneumatic tubing damage could be compared to what would happen to a human if the connections were severed from the brain to the various body organs. If the fire had been planned, a worse location could not have been picked. In assessing the fire damage, it was discovered that almost all of the wiring and tubing had been burned through. And there were literally thousands of these wires and tubes. Even those that had not been destroyed would need to be replaced since it was likely that they might have been damaged. Frank Baron immediately put the instrument start-up team on twelve-hour shifts. Massey Chemical was now losing money on a plant that was not making product. The repairs needed to be done quickly and be totally checked before starting up. Essentially, the entire plant had to be rewired and retubed.

The instrument and electrical engineers discussed several solutions, but the one selected was to install about fifty new electrical and pneumatic junction boxes up in the pipe rack, on the field side of the burned area. The field wires and tubes would then be pulled in from the undamaged area and terminated in the new junction boxes on the field side of the burned area. On the other side of the fire, the tubes ran into the control room and terminated on various terminal strips and tubing tees; therefore, since the distance was short, these wires and tubes would eventually be completely rerun from the control room to the new junction boxes.

Before the control room wiring and tubing work could proceed, new cable tray, conduits, wiring bundles, and tubing bundles would need to be run across the fire area between the control room and the new junction boxes. Once completed, that would allow the wires and tubes to be terminated on the control room terminals and tees and in the new junction boxes, reestablishing the original prefire connections. In layman's terms, the plant wiring and tubing would be "rerun" across the fire gap—the nerves would be reconnected from the brain to the body organs. Sounds simple, but it would take at least three months to do the work and thoroughly check everything out.

An investigation team was formed to determine the root cause of the fire. After several weeks it was determined that high-voltage, high-current electrical equipment's conduit and wiring had been run near lower-voltage control wiring, although on different pipe rack levels. It is normal practice to separate these on the pipe racks to avoid electrical noise. It was deduced that one of the high-voltage circuits had overloaded or short-circuited, causing the fire. In turn, this had burned through the lower-voltage wiring and tubing. But why hadn't the electrical equipment sensed this short circuit and tripped the breaker? In the motor control center (MCC), the investigation revealed that someone had blocked the electrical breaker in the ON position with a foot long wooden four-by-four-inch piece of lumber so that when a trip occurred, it could not open the electrical circuit. This was attributed by the investigating team to some contractor making a dumb mistake. In tracing down that particular circuit, it was found that it went to a boiler feedwater pump motor that had been mechanically prevented from turning by jamming a piece of six-inch pipe under the motor/pump coupling. The wiring was correctly sized for the expected load; however, on any motor, "locked rotor current" is extremely high—close to a short circuit. Since the electrical trip had been blocked, when an attempt to start the feedwater pump was made, electrical current went sky-high, burned through the wiring insulation, shorted to ground through the conduit, and the fire was a foregone result. The resulting fire burned through other conduits and wiring, contributing to the fire.

When Bob heard this conclusion, he immediately thought of the man in the aluminum hard hat who appeared to be sneaking into the MCC and later was running/limping away from it. He remembered that the jammed boiler feedwater pump was located adjacent to the pipe rack leading to the control room, and close to the MCC. Again, he mentioned his concerns to Frank Baron, but he dismissed Bob's "tin man" as an unlikely candidate.

Frank said, *"After all, how many chemical plant fires are caused by arsonists? It is much easier to burn down a warehouse filled with paper products."*

Bob thought, *One coincidence (the blocked electrical trip) might have been a mistake, but two coincidences (the blocked pump motor) strains credulity!*

Bob might have eventually agreed with Frank if the electrical fire was the only incident.

Unfortunately, Frank's characterization of the Tin Man began to spread around the plant, and people began to kid Bob about it.

"Hey, Bob, wasn't the Tin Man looking for a brain? How about clicking your ruby slippers together—to go back to Ohio."

Fortunately, Bob had a thick skin, and he would shoot back, *"Good idea—we never burned down the Bell Park plant! Maybe you guys need to buy some life insurance!"*

No one but Bob believed this was arson—but facts have a way of winning the day.

CHAPTER 3

PROBLEMS, PROBLEMS, ALL DAY LONG

For the next three months, everyone's effort was concentrated on rewiring and retubing the plant through the fire-damaged area. This could be compared to a neurosurgeon reconnecting every nerve from a human's brain to the rest of the body. The electrical fire had been in the worst place possible—where all wiring and tubing entered the control building. Even after this work was done, the instrument folks would have to swing into action and check every signal to and from the control room. Bear in mind, this had all been done before, prior to the fire, but now every signal had to be checked again before the plant could attempt a restart. This was quickly becoming one of the longest and costliest start-ups in Massey Chemical's history. Massey's stock price had dropped by 20 percent. Massey folks saw their IRA's falling in value, and there were not many happy campers.

Finally, after three months, the day arrived when the final connection had been tested, and the plant began to restart. They were finally back to where they were prior to the fire. Fred Conway was busy assisting where needed on the start-up of the three high-pressure boilers. This particular type of boiler firing controls had never been used before by Massey Chemical. They consisted of solid-state logic elements on printed circuit boards, with the logic determined by cross wiring between the boards. At the time this was leading-edge technology. Within a few years, it would be replaced by programmable logic controllers, where the cross wiring would be done in the software. But at this time, the instrument technicians were in the learning phase.

To be kind, things were not going well. The boilers kept shutting down, "for no good reason," according to the technicians. Since this was not Bob Garver's area, he found Fred Conway's predicament a bit humorous. It seemed like every day at about 3:00 p.m., the huge high-pressure relief valve on one of the boilers would trip open, dumping 1,200 PSIG steam to the atmosphere and producing a sound similar to a 747 jet revving up in your driveway. It happened so often that Fred would put his head down on his desk, awaiting Bud Asperson, the utilities manager, to come stomping into the start-up trailer.

Bud would yell, *"Conway, your d*** instrument techs shut my boiler down again!"*

Fred would put on his hard hat and head out to find out what had happened this time. Generally, it turned out that Bud was right—Fred's instrument tech had made some mistake and shut the system down. That, coupled with the fact that the boiler firing control designers had used some rather complex control strategies, and the operators did not fully understand them.

Unfortunately, these boiler shutdowns happened so frequently, upper management informed the start-up team leader, Frank Baron, that it was time for him to retire. Massey stock was now down 30 percent from its pre-start-up high. Money was pouring out of Massey's coffers like the Niagara River over Niagara Falls! Everybody working for Frank Baron liked him, so this was a blow to the morale of the start-up team.

Frank had been in the instrumentation business since the beginning of time. Bob Garver remembered one corporate instrument meeting he attended in New York City where a young whippersnapper instrument engineer questioned what Frank was saying about differential pressure transmitters.

Frank looked across the table at him and said, *"Son, I've repaired more differential pressure transmitters than you have even seen. Try listening and learning instead of talking!"*

A bit rough, but he was accurate on the point he was making. He was also known for becoming a wild man on company trips. On one occasion, also in New York City, he got mugged.

In relating the story, he said that he told the mugger, *"My wallet is in my right-hand suit pocket—just leave me money for a taxi."*

The crook did.

At Frank's retirement party, held in the start-up team trailer, Frank pulled the three team leaders into his office, opened his desk drawer, and offered them a shot of whiskey. This was totally against Massey policy, but they all toasted him and wished him luck in retirement. And after all, what could Massey do to him? They had already put him out to pasture. Frank would be missed.

The pyrolysis area instrument engineer, Jack Fishbane, was appointed to take Frank's place as start-up team leader. He would also continue his previous responsibilities—following the pyrolysis area start-up of eight (8) furnaces, the gasoline hydrotreater unit, and the butadiene unit. Unlike Frank Baron, Jack was not liked by everyone on the start-up team. He was demanding, and had a way of cutting people down a notch when dealing with them. As an example, the first day in his new position, he drew up a level transmitter application complete with dimensions, specific gravity, and fill fluid gravity, and told Bob Garver to calculate the range of the transmitter. Jack was an old Southern boy, and he wanted to make sure this Yankee from Ohio knew what he was doing. He watched as Bob made the calculations—talk about pressure! Whew! He got it right!

Few liked Jack, but he was the right person to address the boiler shutdown issue.

Jack's first order was *"NO WORK will be done on ANY boiler shutdown system unless a Massey Chemical instrument engineer is present supervising the work!"*

Needless to say, this did not sit well with the start-up team since it meant they would be called out at any hour of the day or night to supervise work on the boiler shutdown systems. On the other hand, Jack solved the problem—the mysterious boiler shutdowns stopped! Fred Conway no longer had to apologize to the utilities manager every afternoon. And it was discovered that instrument engineers can exist without much sleep!

Early one morning around 3:00 a.m., there were problems that the operators thought were associated with one of the boiler shutdown systems. Harold Neymeir was on call to supervise any boiler shutdown system work. A couple of years earlier, Harold had transferred from an overseas company into Massey. He spoke with a slight German accent. Harold had been called out on other unrelated problems the last three nights, and he was beat. Each instrument engineer was supplied with a "beeper" that would respond with a beep when its particular phone number was called. Harold had been "beeped" multiple times before the operators gave up and called Jack Fishbane. Jack came out to the plant and solved their problem. However, he was waiting for Harold when he came in the next morning.

He loudly asked, *"Neymeir, why didn't you answer your beeper last night!"*

In a fake German accent, Harold said, *"Ya vol mein commandant! Sorry, Jack, I didn't hear it. Maybe I was out of range or something."*

Later, Bob Garver asked him about it.

He said, *"Bob, it's really hard to hear the beeper when it is under your mattress."*

Jack never found out.

On another occasion, a local instrument vendor invited the instrument engineers to a shrimp boil. This involved boiling a bazillion shrimp in their shells, using highly spiced water. There were other foods, but shrimp was the main drawing card. Bob Garver and Jack attended, and Jack brought his wife. The procedure was to strain the shrimp out of the water and throw them out on the table, which was lined with old newspapers. Then the hungry shrimp eaters would peel the shrimp and eat them. Delicious! No deveining—just peel and eat them poop and all. Bob dug in and looked like he was going for the record. But Jack wouldn't peel the shrimp—too much work and too messy. Instead, he had his wife peel them for him. It revealed how meticulous Jack was, and why he was so thin, but Bob couldn't help pitying his wife. Later in his career, Jack got assigned to start-up teams on a regular basis since he developed a reputation for being so detail oriented, catching every possible start-up problem.

Now that reliable steam was available, various parts of the olefins complex began their start-up procedures. Just north of the control room was a high-pressure hydrogen heat exchanger. Somehow, during one afternoon, a leak developed and hydrogen caught fire at a flange. It is interesting that hydrogen burns with a pale-blue flame that is nearly invisible in daylight. Also, a pure hydrogen flame will not produce smoke, so the fire went undetected for about an hour, and it destroyed the leaking flange and some of the pipe close by, making the leak even bigger. Hydrogen flames may appear yellow if there are impurities in the surrounding air, like dust or other chemicals. Fortunately, in this case, chemical plants are not known for their ultrapure air, so the fire was eventually discovered and extinguished. Investigation showed that the flange bolts on the exchanger had been loose. Again, the relatively small fire was attributed to poor checkout by the contractor.

While this fire was being put out, an operator was walking down under the main pipe rack. He heard a loud screaming noise, which seemed to come from the area around the high-pressure steam letdown valve. Most people think of steam as being visible, and it is at normal pressures; however, at high pressure, it is invisible at the point of escape, becoming visible only when its temperature and pressure drops, and this can occur quite a way away from the source of the leak. Old-timers like this particular operator know this, and he blocked off the area and found a broom to search for the leak. He quickly discovered that steam was coming from the letdown valve flanges—as the broom passed the leak, it got chopped to bits. Much better than having an arm or leg chopped off; brooms are cheap—body parts, not so. Here again, it was discovered that the bolts on the flanges had been loose. Poor checkout by the contractor? That was becoming harder to believe.

Bob Garver was beginning to wonder whether he needed more life insurance or a ticket back to Ohio.

Jack Fishbane told him, *"You are in a chemical plant! What do you expect when you heat up gasoline with fire and boil it? It's dangerous!"*

Not too comforting! Massey stock dropped another 5 percent. In these cases, the damage was relatively easy to fix, and the plant was again ready for start-up within two days. A few weeks went by without any more incidents. But the brief respite was short-lived.

The pyrolysis furnaces were being started up, producing cracked gas that needed to be pressured up in two process gas compressors. Essentially pyrolysis takes high molecular hydrocarbons and heats the heck out of them until they "crack" into lighter hydrocarbons. Basically, the long chemical chains are broken into pieces by the intense heat. Things were going great—process gas was being produced—and it was time to start one of the process gas compressors. Unfortunately, "someone" had left a three-inch block valve open on one of the compressor knockout vessels, and when process gas was introduced, it started exhausting through that valve. At high pressure, a huge amount of gas can escape from a three-inch block valve. Three things are required to start a fire: fuel (there was now lots of that), air (lots of that to breathe and to mix with the fuel), and an ignition source (remember those furnaces?). Within minutes, the leaking process gas, mixed with air, found its way to the fires in a pyrolysis furnace, and BOOM!

All the windows were shattered in the start-up team trailer; and even in the administration building, a quarter of a mile away, a few were blown out. Fortunately, the control room was windowless, and the operators were able to bring the plant down (*again*). In addition, the compressor shutdown system functioned properly, and the operators were able to shut it down, removing the source of the gas. Also, it should be noted that most start-ups occur during the night shift so that fewer people are exposed. This probably saved the instrument folks since they were home—and the start-up trailer was empty.

When Bob Garver came to work the next morning, he was amazed at the damage. His office was a mess with papers blown all over the room. There were no windows left in the trailer, and shards of glass were everywhere. Power was out, so there was no air-conditioning (essential in Houston). So he went out to the field to find out what had happened. He quickly learned that, unfortunately, one of the operators, Mike Bourne, had been in the area when the explosion occurred. The resulting fire prevented anyone from getting to him quickly. By the time they got him out, Mike was dead—badly burned, with most of his bones broken—a grizzly sight.

The area containing process gas compressor 1 was a disaster. Similar to the earlier wiring and tubing incident outside the control room, the explosion and resulting fire had destroyed much of the wiring and tubing in the compressor area. Cable trays that carried the wiring and tubing had been blown completely out of the pipe rack and scattered across the plant. Some smaller process pipes were bent, but fortunately did not rupture. The area of the explosion looked like a war zone. It would have to be completely redone.

This was the third major event. The olefins plant would remain down for another two months. Massey stock reached an all-time low, 45 percent below its pre-start-up high. Money was supposed to be rolling in—not rolling out!

Someone was dead! Two operators insisted they both had checked that block valve, and it was checked as closed on the pre-start-up checklist. Block valves don't just open by themselves. And looking back, without help, electrical motor starters don't get jammed open at the same time a motor coupling is kept from rotating. In addition, high-pressure hydrogen pipe flanges and high-pressure steam flanges don't loosen themselves! All these "coincidences" led Massey management to bring in the Deer Park Police to investigate. As Leroy Jethro Gibbs says on *NCIS*, *"Rule 39: There is no such thing as a coincidence."* In addition, OSHA (Occupational Safety and Health Administration) came down on Massey with both feet. Now the government was involved—never a good thing.

CHAPTER 4

THE INVESTIGATION BEGINS

Betty Marcum was a pretty blond woman that stood 6'2" tall, with shoulder-length hair tied in a bun behind her police cap. She was the investigating police officer assigned to the Massey Arson Case. Criminals who decided to give her a hard time soon found out that was a really bad move! She was born and raised in Pasadena, the city next to Deer Park. After graduating from Texas A&M with a criminal justice degree, she worked her way up through the ranks to her present position as lieutenant. During her ten years on the force, she had taken training in several martial arts and was proficient in karate. Unruly lawbreakers soon found out that she could more than hold her own, and they were soon in handcuffs headed for the pokey. Betty was accompanied by Sergeant Mike Sanchez, a rugged 220-pound police officer with eighteen years on the force. Quite a formidable pair. Working in the Deer Park Police Department, Betty had previous exposure to folks working in the oil and chemical industry, and had learned quite a bit about the refining and chemical business.

After coordinating with Massey Chemical Co. management, the first thing Betty Marcum did was to bring all of the olefins plant personnel into a meeting to explain why they were there and what to expect during the investigation. At one point, she asked the group to contact her if they had any information regarding the fires and explosions. Bob Garver planned to find her as soon as he could to discuss the man in the aluminum hard hat. As one of the first police activities, a forensic team came on-site to look for any evidence that someone was behind these horrible events. They headed out to the sites of the multiple events—the electrical fire outside the control room, the jammed electrical gear, the jammed feedwater pump, the hydrogen flange fire, the high-pressure steam valve leak, and the process gas compressor block valve fire.

Bob Garver had been working for twenty-four hours straight, so following the meeting with the investigators, Jack Fishbane told him to go home and get some sleep.

He said, *"Bob, you look like death warmed over. Go home, and don't come back until tomorrow morning for day shift."*

No need to tell him twice, Bob headed for his apartment, hit the sheets, and didn't wake up until 5:30 a.m. He made a quick stop at the Waffle House for breakfast. He had always liked the informal atmosphere at any Waffle House, and sat at the counter so he could watch his eggs and waffles being made.

Sally, the waitress, knew him from the many times he ate there, and asked him, *"Do you know anything about the explosion at the Massey plant?"* She had seen the fireball from the process gas compressor explosion and was concerned about her safety.

Bob said, *"Sally, not to worry, it is being investigated by the Massey Safety personnel and by the Deer Park Police."* He also said, *"This sort of thing is extremely unusual."*

Sally replied, *"I agree with that—I've lived here for thirty-five years, and this is the first time anything like this has happened."*

After the delicious 2,000-calorie breakfast, complete with lots of butter and syrup on the waffles, Bob got in his beat-up Jeep Cherokee, and arrived in the Massey parking lot around 7:30 a.m.

As he walked down the plant road from the parking lot to the start-up trailer, he thought he might be suffering from an episode of BPPV (benign paroxysmal positional vertigo). A couple of years earlier, he had experienced extreme dizziness, with the world appearing to swirl around him. Any movement made the sensation worse. At the time, this caused him to think he might be having a heart attack or stroke, so he called 911, and an ambulance took him to the emergency room. They did all the normal tests (EKG etc.) and sent him home. Since the dizziness continued, after some Internet research on dizziness, he went to an ear, nose, and throat (ENT) physician who diagnosed him with BPPV.

In some people, usually following some physical trauma, small particles break off in the inner ear and float around. Movement of the head causes these particles to hit against the cilia (small hairs) in the inner ear that normally sense the small movement caused by sound vibrations. The brain sees this "major collision" with a particle, and has no way to interpret it other than thinking the world is coming to an end! It is a terrifying experience. But fortunately, the *B* in BPPV stands for *benign* (nonmalignant), and there is no threat to life, other than the potential for falling. The ENT sent Bob to a physical therapist, and he was introduced to a procedure known as the Epley maneuver. By positioning the head in specific ways, the particles are gradually moved by gravity into an inactive area of the inner ear—thus no impacts, thus no dizziness.

As Bob walked down the olefins plant road to the start-up trailer, he couldn't believe his eyes. Was this an episode of BPPV? He looked to his right where the gasoline hydrotreater (GHT) unit was located. The thirty-foot-diameter cylindrical heater was sloping about twenty degrees to the left, hanging slightly over the road. As he looked closer, he saw that there had been another fire in his absence, and it had burned a large section of the GHT.

This is it, I'm going back to Ohio. This place is going to kill me! Bob thought.

When Bob arrived at the start-up trailer, Jack Fishbane explained that the GHT heater had caught fire overnight. They were investigating the cause. Any hydrotreater, including gasoline hydrotreaters, expose their heated product to high-pressure hydrogen. The purpose, in this case, was to increase the octane value of the gasoline by tacking a hydrogen atom on the end of the shorter cracked hydrocarbon chains. Unfortunately, the heater fire caused a gas escape, and one of the start-up team instrument engineers, Harold Neymeir, had been caught in the gas cloud and collapsed. Fortunately for him, an operator was nearby; he quickly put on a Scott Air-Pak and pulled Harold to safety, saving his life. Once again, the operators managed to shut the unit down, this time without any loss of life.

While walking around the GHT area, Bob ran into Police Lieutenant Betty Marcum. He introduced himself and passed on the information about the man in the aluminum hard hat entering the motor control center (MCC).

"Lieutenant Marcum, it is very unusual for anyone to wear an aluminum hat while working around electrical gear. The MCC is full of electrical gear, and if it makes contact with the aluminum, death is likely. Before safety became a big concern, the old-timers wore this type of hat, but I don't think I have ever seen one in a plant before."

He also told her, *"The guy was limping when he left the MCC, and he ran off as soon as I spotted him. That, too, is unusual—Massey frowns upon running in the plant."*

Lieutenant Marcum asked if he could identify the man.

He told her, *"I was about twenty yards away. The light under the main pipe rack was not that bright, and I only saw his face for about a minute. But I think I might be able to identify him."*

She suggested that he work with a forensic artist to make a sketch. He agreed and asked her to schedule an appointment.

Betty's forensic team had found very little evidence. The MCC cubicle that had been forced open had no fingerprints—it had obviously been wiped clean, or more likely, the culprit wore gloves. Bob got Betty in contact with the start-up team electrical engineer, John Cross, who explained why this blocked contactor, in conjunction with a blocked feedwater pump, caused the fire outside the control room. Both the hydrogen flange fire, the high-pressure steam leak, and the open three-inch block valve fire destroyed most of the evidence that might have been present. However, close by the loose hydrogen flange, they did find a pipe that had some blood and skin on it. Betty theorized that in loosening the flange, the culprit may have "busted his knuckles" while using the large wrench.

They were running the sample's DNA, but it would take a week or so, and there was no proof that it was from the person who loosened the flange. The three-inch block valve fire explosion pretty much removed any evidence that might have been there. The latest fire, in the gasoline hydrotreater unit, was still being investigated. She and Sergeant Sanchez were in the process of interviewing anyone who might have been in the various areas prior to the fires. So far, no luck. However, by this time, the police had concluded that all of these "coincidences" were caused by someone. The hunt was on.

At Betty's request, Bob reported to the Deer Park police station the next day at 10:00 a.m. sharp. Betty introduced Simon Wemple, the forensic sketch artist. They spent the next two hours looking at sketches of facial characteristics to come up with a sketch that represented the man in the aluminum hard hat. Bob remembered that he had a mustache and goatee that blended together. He had wide-set eyes, and he looked mean. The hard hat covered most of his hair, but he remembered that it was dark black, and that he had long sideburns. Bob estimated that he was five feet and nine or ten inches tall by comparing his height with the seven-foot-tall MCC door that he used to exit the building. Although it had been dark, he thought he saw a long scar across the man's right cheek, down toward his mouth. The artist made his sketch, and then made several changes based on Bob's suggestions. The final product was pretty good in Bob's estimation. The sketch was placed on all of the Massey bulletin boards and circulated to the local papers. It never occurred to Bob that he had now become the only "witness" that could convict this arsonist.

The repairs to the GHT unit heater area were extensive. Instruments, tubing, and wiring had been burned up over a twenty-by-twenty-yard area. The heater had experienced extensive damage inside and out, and its support structural steel framework would need to be replaced where it had failed.

Even though the GHT unit was in Jack Fishbane's area, because of Bob Garver's previous work experience, Jack asked Bob to assist him with the GHT instrument replacements. Bob called his contacts at his old employer, Moore Products Company. He asked them to give Massey fast, top-notch service, since Moore was being called on to replace the destroyed field instrumentation. Most instrument manufacturers will bend over backward to help a customer when they have had an explosion or fire. Moore still had the specifications for the originally supplied instruments, so they quickly quoted them, and Bob got them a purchase order in record time.

Moore made this their first priority, moving these required instruments to the head of the production line. They had the instrumentation built and shipped within six weeks, a remarkable achievement since normal delivery was twelve to sixteen weeks. It took another four weeks to install the instruments. Fortunately, most process pipes were large enough in diameter that they survived the fire. Since the cable trays in the pipe rack approaching the burned-out heater had been melted, they had to be replaced.

The GHT heater rebuild followed the same strategy that was being used on the other units; tubing and wiring were terminated in new terminal boxes and junction boxes just outside of the burned-out area. Then the rest of the field wiring and tubing were run to the instruments from the new boxes. Fortunately, there were a few existing boxes that were not impacted by the fire, and some of the field wires and tubing did not need to be replaced. This work was scheduled during the time the new instruments and structural steel were being manufactured and delivered. The olefins "start-up" project had once again become a "construction" project. Massey stock took another hit. Employees, regarding their IRAs, began sadly joking, *"How low can it go?"*

The investigation of the GHT heater fire had produced some results. They found more "coincidences." Bob Garver explained the start-up procedure to Lieutenant Betty Marcum.

"The natural gas supply to the heater is equipped with two valves, a solenoid valve-operated shutdown valve and a control valve that has a manual reset shutdown solenoid installed. In addition, the area between the two valves has a small solenoid-equipped valve that vents this space to the flare system in the event of a shutdown to make sure any leak in the upstream valve cannot reach the heater. During start-up of the heater, the small vent valve is powered up to close it—then, after a short time delay, the shutdown valve solenoid is powered up to open its shutdown valve. At this point, the manual reset solenoid on the control valve is powered on, but is not yet reset.

"The next step is for the control room operator to adjust the natural gas pressure controller to light off position. At that point, the field operator can lift the manual reset solenoid lever, allowing gas to flow to the heater burners. He then energizes the sparking device to light the burners, visually confirming the flame stability. The heater can then be put on gas pressure control. After pressure is established and stabilized, the pressure control can be put in 'cascade' mode where the heater exit temperature controller sets the set point of the natural gas pressure."

Bob noted that this start-up procedure had occurred normally prior to the fire. He explained that if any of the shutdown events occurred, the three solenoid valves would be depowered, and air would be vented from these three valves. At this point, the shutdown valve and control valve were supposed to close, and the area between them would vent to the flare (to handle any tiny leaks through the upstream valve). Betty thanked Bob for the explanation and remarked that it sounded awfully complex.

Bob said, *"That's why they pay me the big bucks!"* and both of them laughed.

Betty described to Bob what the investigation had found. The two heater exit temperature transmitters had their thermocouples removed from their thermowells. Bob explained that this would cause the control transmitter to only sense ambient temperature. It would think the heater had gone cold. This would result in the exit temperature controller calling for the maximum amount of natural gas pressure. And since the exit temperature shutdown transmitter had also been removed, it could not respond to the resulting high heater temperature.

Bob said, *"Thermocouples don't remove themselves!"*

But Bob wondered—there was a high-pressure shutdown—why had that not prevented the overfiring? They both went to look at this shutdown. As they walked over, Bob explained that the shutdown pressure transmitter should have sensed the high gas pressure and caused a shutdown. Apparently, the investigating team had missed the fact that the shutdown pressure transmitter had been blocked in.

Bob commented, *"Betty, because of the removed thermocouples, to the shutdown system, the heater looked 'cool,' not hot—and when it called for maximum gas firing, the high-pressure shutdown thought things were fine because it was blocked in."*

Betty asked, *"But weren't there other shutdown devices?"*

Bob had a set of P&IDs (process and instrumentation drawings) that he used to show her.

He indicated, *"There were skin temperature thermocouples welded to the surfaces of the heater tubes, but these were only alarm devices."*

Betty said, *"The records showed that several of these alarms had indicated high temperature, but the operators were occupied with other issues related to the fire."*

Bob said, *"I understand that—when you are up to your neck in alligators, there's not time to discuss draining the swamp. And they assumed the shutdown system would do its job!"*

Bob's description explained why the heater controls sent high natural gas pressure to the burners. That would explain the high exit temperature. But Betty asked what would cause the major fire inside and outside the heater.

Bob theorized, *"The purpose of this heater is to heat the process using natural gas. But in a sense, the heated process stream also carries away the heat so that the heater tubes will not melt. An example of that would be firing the heater without any liquid in the tubes—that would result in melting the tubes. And during the GHT unit start-up, the process flow was intentionally at a low rate, not carrying much heat away. If the unit had been at design flow rate, the heater might have survived without tube failure. But in fact, the combination of the low product flow rate and the maximum gas firing probably caused the product to start vaporizing, which reduced the 'heat carry away' even further, since heat transfer is more efficient from liquid to liquid than it is from gas to gas."*

Betty said, *"It was sort of like the perfect storm—everything went wrong at the same time."*

Bob mentioned another factor: *"At normal firing rates, the natural gas flames do not impinge on the heater tubes. However, at the wide-open gas flow rate, the flames likely impinged on the lower tubes. The tube metallurgy is not designed for this case. I visualize the lower tubes initially glowing red, then white, and finally one failed. A hole developed, allowing the process hydrocarbon to flow into the combustion chamber, and this set the entire firebox ablaze. With the firebox engulfed in flames, other tubes began to fail, and I suspect it didn't take long for the firebox itself to be breached, causing the fires up the sides of the heater."*

Betty said, *"All these things could not have happened without human intervention. There is no question, there is an arsonist on the loose, and he is out to get Massey for some reason."*

Betty explained that the investigation had revealed that the problem was finally detected during the night shift when a field operator was walking through the plant and noticed that the GHT heater had flames licking up the side of the heater. He used the GHT unit natural gas manual-block valve to close off the gas, but noticed that the fire continued to burn. This would have been the liquid hydrocarbon from the tubes still feeding the fire. The operator radioed the control room, and they shut off the hydrocarbon feed. But by that time, the heater was a total loss, along with much of the surrounding equipment.

Betty commented to Bob, *"Coincidence number 150? I think not!"*

Apparently, the man who had by now been dubbed the Tin Man was hurried in his arson efforts, or was getting sloppy. The forensic team found partial fingerprints on the thermocouples that he removed, and apparently he cut his finger when isolating the low-pressure shutdown transmitter, leaving some blood on the valve. The DNA from the hydrogen flange fire was back, but unfortunately did not match anyone in the DNA database. But the blood sample from this latest fire was sent out for DNA analysis and comparison. This could prove the fires were caused by the same individual.

It had been a very good day for Betty. Her investigating team had discovered the causes of the fire. There was absolutely no doubt that this was arson. She now understood the causes of the fire, and the partial fingerprint and blood samples might help pin down the suspect. And it was becoming increasingly obvious that the arsonist had a background in instrumentation since most people would have no idea how to disable a complicated shutdown system like he had.

Bob commented to Betty, *"You may want to put me on the suspect list—the arsonist is obviously someone who has instrumentation experience."*

Betty laughed and said, *"Yeah, you do look guilty!"*

*   *   *

Bob had found out from Sergeant Sanchez that Betty was not married, so he risked asking her to have dinner with him. She surprised him by saying yes, since she was 6'2" tall, and he was only 6' tall. His insecurity made him think that she "towered" over him.

The GHT unit fire had caused Massey stock to take another hit. People were beginning to "panic sell," and this only added to the drop in price. Would these problems ever end?

CHAPTER 5

THE ATTACK

Bob decided to go all out for his dinner with Betty. He made reservations at Purdy's Steak House on the Gulf Freeway. He got out his best "Sunday go to meeting" suit and spent thirty minutes trying to decide on a tie. When he picked her up at 7:30 p.m., she was wearing a simple Kelly green dress with a pearl necklace. His expression told her that he was blown away.

He stammered, *"You-you-you look great, Betty!"*

On the way to the restaurant, Bob tried to learn more about Betty. She indicated that she lived in a Pasadena apartment complex with a roommate, Cindy Parker. She attended a local nondenominational church and was quite serious about her relationship with Christ. This pleased Bob since he was also a dedicated Christian. He found out that she had a small Shih Tzu dog named Robber and a cat named Bandit (both of which seemed appropriate for a police officer). She liked country music and travelled whenever her salary and time allowed. They both had been to some of the same places, like the Grand Canyon and Disney World.

Conversation was easy, and it seemed like no time had passed when they arrived at Purdy's. They were shown to a table in the center of the restaurant, but Betty asked if they could have the table that was against the wall, facing the entrance.

After they sat down, Bob asked, *"Why do you prefer this table?"*

She said, *"I learned that in police training. If a shooter comes in, I would quickly be able to identify the problem and deal with it. If I was facing away, or in a section of the restaurant where the entrance was not visible, it would take precious seconds to react, and people might die unnecessarily."*

Bob had never thought of that, but it made sense.

It caused him to ask Betty, *"Are you carrying a weapon tonight?"*

She laughed and said, *"Yes, but you can't see where I'm hiding it."*

He laughed, and let her know that he had a concealed handgun permit (after all, this was Texas), and that he presently had a small Ruger 9 mm in a shoulder holster under his jacket.

He joked, *"After all, I might need it tonight to defend myself from you."*

They both laughed, and then talked about guns for a while.

Dinner went remarkably well, considering this was their first date. Bob had the famous Purdy pork chops, which were essentially made from an entire pork roast, sliced up. Betty ordered a petit filet. Both dinners came with a house tossed salad and steamed vegetables. For dessert they shared a bananas foster, which was delicious.

*   *   *

Both of them asked for doggie bags to take the extra food home.

Betty remarked, *"A cop taking food home to a Robber and a Bandit just doesn't seem right."*

Bob said, *"I'll bet you will eat more of the remaining steak than either Robber or Bandit."*

Betty just smiled.

He then said, *"I have no plans to share my pork chops with my tropical fish."*

Bob had always had at least one tropical fish tank, ever since college. He told her that he presently had a thirty-gallon freshwater tank with parrot fish, those big orange circular fish. However, he noted, *"I'm pretty sure that their mouths won't go around a pork chop."*

As they were laughing, the waiter brought the bill; Bob ordered coffee for them and gave him his Visa card. After signing, they continued to enjoy the coffee and talked for a while until the waiter started "circling." Betty noticed that the restaurant was filling up and that they needed the table, so they decided to leave.

On the ride back to Betty's apartment, the conversation turned to the fires and explosions at the Massey olefins plant. She said she hoped that both DNA samples were from the Tin Man—to prove that it was a single arsonist. To Bob's chagrin, now even the police were referring to him as the Tin Man. Unfortunately, they had found no match for the first sample in the DNA database, but Betty indicated that they were now researching other databases. When and if they came up with a suspect, these samples could be part of the evidence needed to convict.

She indicated that Bob's sketch of the culprit wearing the aluminum hat was probably the best identification evidence they had at this point. The sketch had been circulated around the plant, posted on every bulletin board, and published twice in the local newspaper, asking readers to help identify the arsonist. As typical, the newspaper sensationalized it by referring to him as the Tin Man. Anything to increase circulation! It was becoming apparent that the name had stuck, and it wasn't going to change. A few tips had come in, but the people had solid alibis. Betty cautioned Bob that he should be careful, since he was the only witness that could identify the bad guy; and since Tin Man obviously had access to the plant, he would have seen the sketch. Bob laughed it off.

Bob dropped Betty off at her apartment complex, telling her that he had enjoyed the evening immensely. She said she had a great time too, and suggested they might do it again soon. It was a short drive from Pasadena to Bob's Deer Park apartment. He pulled into his normal parking spot, got out, and locked the car, heading for the stairs to his second-floor apartment.

Suddenly, he sensed something was wrong. He couldn't put a name on it, but as *Spider-Man* would say, *"His Spidey senses went up."* As he approached the stairs, he saw a shadow move from behind the stairs and start toward him, holding what appeared to be a long hunting knife. The attacker had a ski mask over his face.

Immediately Bob drew his 9 mm Ruger and shouted, *"Stop, I have a gun!"*

Reminiscent of Indiana Jones, he thought, *"Never take a knife to a gunfight!"*

At this point, the attacker decided he was a lover, not a fighter, and turned tail, running out of the parking lot. Sure enough, the man had a pronounced limp—it was the Tin Man for sure. Bob ran after him, but lost him in the maze of apartments. He went to his apartment and called 911, asking for them to alert Lieutenant Betty Marcum.

Deer Park police are generally very efficient, and they had a patrol car at the apartment complex within ten minutes. A short time after, Betty arrived in her personal car. Bob immediately showed them his concealed handgun permit and handed Betty his gun (no magazine and slide open) to make the police feel more comfortable. He explained how the knife attack occurred and that threatening the attacker with his gun caused the bad guy to run off. Betty was especially interested that he wore a ski mask, and the fact that he limped as he ran off—but she resisted irritating Bob by calling him the Tin Man. Obviously, this was the same man who was causing the Massey Chemical fires and explosions; and his intent had been to eliminate the only witness who could identify him. The police put up a perimeter around the apartment complex, but with no results. They questioned many of the apartment complex dwellers, but none had seen the attack since it was late at night.

Betty jokingly asked Bob, *"Do you want me to stay the night to protect you?"*

He said, *"No thanks, I will be sleeping with my 9 mm for company. And we better protect our reputations."*

There was little chance the culprit would reappear that night. But unknown to Bob, Betty had a police patrol car check on the apartment complex frequently during the night. It was apparent the "fondness" that was developing was two-way. The rest of the night was uneventful.

The next day at work, the attack was the topic of conversation everywhere because it had made the TV news. Bob had become an overnight celebrity!

A couple of the instrument engineers started calling him Clint Eastwood or Harry Callahan, telling him, *"Make my day."*

This was certainly better than the Tin Man moniker and the *Wizard of Oz* references with which he had previously been saddled.

He usually replied with a Clint Eastwood accent, *"I'm more the Lone Ranger type! Wanna see my silver bullets?"*

Bob's organization of the GHT unit fire zone rebuild was allowing it to proceed nicely. There was plenty to occupy everyone's time since materials were being ordered, delivered, and installed as fast as possible. After finalizing the purchase order with Moore Products, Bob had focused on getting all of the tubing and electrical wiring drawings marked up to show the junction box changes so they could be sent to drafting for correction. The OSHA (Occupational Safety and Health Administration) inspection had not turned up any major safety concerns, and they had concluded these events were a police matter.

*   *   *

Betty Marcum was investigating potential tips resulting from the artist's sketch. The forensic team had found no obvious evidence at the scene of the previous night's attack, which was no surprise since the Tin Man had been wearing gloves. They did collect a few hair samples, for DNA analysis, and had found a few other dropped items, but the odds that they came from the culprit were pretty small since this was a highly travelled area in the apartment complex.

Betty had come up with a couple of other possible items to investigate. For example, she wondered if anyone had been fired from Massey Chemical in the last year? Or had any of the various contractors' folks been disciplined lately? Were there any company/union disputes that might have caused this level of revenge? Also, the Massey folks needed to be reinterviewed to see if they knew of anyone who was very upset with the company. And her focus had started to shift toward "instrument" people because of the technical know-how used to cause the GHT unit fire. All of this took time. But so far, no results.

Again, Betty warned Bob to watch his step, since the Tin Man seemed to have unlimited access to the plant and had demonstrated his ability to get close and attack. Betty thought that it was likely the culprit was regularly employed at Massey, or had been, because of his familiarity with the plant. Bob suggested to Betty that the individual would probably be older rather than younger based on the aluminum hard hat. Workers had not worn metal hats for many years. This also made him question Betty's idea that he was employed at the plant since he would have worn the Massey-issued plastic hard hat. Bob suggested that he probably had shaved off his facial hair by now and that the sketch artist might make a revised drawing. She might also see if any of the workers at Massey had recently changed their facial appearance, and see if anyone had a large scar across their right cheek, which he was reasonably sure he had seen on the Tin Man at the MCC.

Then Bob had a brainstorm. He suggested that Betty determine if anyone had recently sold a large amount of Massey stock "short," since the company stock had dropped almost 50 percent in value. He explained that selling a stock short is essentially betting that a stock's value will go down rather than up. To sell a stock short, you follow four steps:

1. Find the stock you want to bet against.
2. Ask the broker to find shares of the stock you think will go down (in this case Massey Chemical), and request to borrow the shares—this is usually done in a broker "margin" account.
3. The broker then locates an investor who owns the shares and borrows them with a promise to return the shares at a prearranged later date, with a small profit.
4. Hopefully, the value of the stock "shorted" drops like a rock (a good description of Massey stock).
5. Lastly, you buy the stock at the low value and use the low-priced stock to "return" the high-priced shares you borrowed.

Bob explained another way to look at it. *"You borrow high and return low—the opposite of the simple stock rule: 'buy low, sell high.'"*

But he explained that selling short is fraught with high risk. If the shorted stock goes up instead of down, you still have to buy the borrowed stock back at a higher price than you borrowed it for. And worse yet, there is no real ceiling regarding how high a stock can go. Normally when you buy a stock, the most you can lose is 100 percent of what you bought it for. With shorted stock, there is no limit to your possible losses—for example, the stock could triple, and you would lose 200 percent.

But Bob explained, *"If you know a stock is going to drop, for greedy people it becomes tempting to 'short' the stock. However, people who know a stock is going to drop in value are theoretically prevented from using 'insider trading' to make money. The Security and Exchange Commission (SEC) frowns on this activity, and you can go to jail for it. Nevertheless, the temptation of huge profits can be great."*

Betty questioned, *"Is that a reason for anyone to burn down a chemical plant and end up killing someone?"*

Bob told her, *"There are people with tens of thousands of Massey shares—worth millions. A short sale where the stock drops 40–50 percent could bring out the sinful nature present in mankind."*

Betty said, *"But would that person try to kill you as the witness?"*

Bob noted, *"As a policewoman, you are aware that there are hit men who will do just about anything for money—there would be no reason for the large stockholder to get his hands dirty."*

Betty agreed to look into it.

For the next three months, the repair efforts continued. No additional attacks occurred, and it almost seemed like it had been a bad dream.

CHAPTER 6

HEAD OFFICE

Bob Garver's agreement to accept the transfer from the Massey Ohio Bell Park plant to Houston was with the understanding that he would be assigned to Massey's head office engineering following the olefins plant start-up. Because the rebuilding was going so well, and it would take at least three months for the olefins plant damaged areas to be ready to start again, Bob was temporarily moved to Massey's head office Engineering, and would return to Deer Park when the plant was ready for start-up.

Unfortunately, head office was located in downtown Houston, which meant a difficult commute. A five-minute commute to the Deer Park plant changed to a one-hour commute each way. Bob's new boss would be Ralph Swenson, a customer he used to call on at Massey's Wood Creek, New Jersey, plant when he was in sales for Moore Products Company. He had used Ralph as a reference when applying for the job at Massey. Ralph had a high opinion of Bob, primarily because he got taken to lunch frequently. Ralph was of the opinion that the chef at the Wood Creek Golf Course restaurant made the best onion soup in the world, so generally, that is where they went for lunch. Ralph smoked big green cigars—back in the day when smoking was allowed just about everywhere. When he wasn't smoking one, he was chewing on one.

Because projects handled at head office took from two to three years to complete, Bob could not be assigned to a new project. Therefore, he was given "small stuff" to work on, like reviewing specification sheets for other instrument engineers. It was "busy work"—but then, it was only for three months. During his three years at the Massey Bell Park plant, he had used his spare time to learn FORTRAN programming. Time-share computing was in vogue at the time, where various customers would "dial in" over phone lines to a vendor-owned computer to run their programs. It seems archaic today, but the program was typed into a teletype terminal and saved on a roll of yellow paper tape about an inch wide. As the programmer typed, the tape had holes punched across it. Which holes got punched determined the information stored.

Anyway, Bob had used this method to program orifice calculations. An orifice is essentially a plate with a hole in the center. The process stream flows through this hole, and by measuring the differential pressure across the orifice, you can determine the flow rate. These calculations were rather laborious to do by hand. He then took a further step and made the program "conversational." This meant that the program would ask questions on the teletype, and the engineer would type in the answers. For example, *"What is the maximum flow rate?" "What is the specific gravity?" etc.* This made running orifice calculations quite simple. The program could also be used in "batch mode" for large projects, where data for multiple orifices could be read in from paper tape at one time. Then the computer would run calculations for all the orifice plates, printing the results without further attention.

While Bob was at Deer Park on the olefins plant start-up, the contractor engineers had run all of the orifice calculations. They used another archaic method—punched cards. When you wanted to run a calculation, you asked a technician to type the information in on a card punch device. Then, you took the stack of punched cards to a computer technician, who fed them into the computer, and the result was a calculation. The computer was usually backed up, and it generally took twenty-four hours to get the calculation. That was not a big deal at the plant since they didn't run many orifice calculations; but on a head office project, with many orifice calculations, this was a hassle.

Fortunately, head office had access to the same time-share computer that Bob used at Bell Park. He called his old boss at Bell Park and asked him to have a copy of the orifice program paper tape mailed to him. When the tape arrived, he fed it into the time-share computer under the head office account, and began to use it for orifice calculations. He told the other head office instrument engineers, and it wasn't long before everyone was using this method since it was so much more efficient. Although generally their contractors ran the project orifice calculations, the head office engineers started using the program to spot-check the results.

But then Bob made a "political" mistake. His buddies at the olefins plant learned that this method existed and asked Bob for a copy so that they could avoid the twenty-four-hour delay using the punch cards. No problem—he made a copy of the tape and mailed it out to Deer Park. Again, the program received praise for how much more efficient it was compared to the old method.

Somehow, Ralph Swenson learned that Bob had sent the program to the plant. Boom!

He stormed into Bob's office and loudly shouted, *"You NEVER send anything from head office to any plant location without my approval. It MUST go up the head office chain of command and down through the operations chain of command!"*

Bob waited for the explosion to subside, and he explained the fact that this method of calculation would save Massey lots of money, and that the plant instrument engineers loved it.

Ralph did not even listen to the arguments, he just said, *"Don't you EVER do that again!"* and stormed out of the office.

Historically, Bob was known to overreact. As an example, one time at the Bell Park plant, someone had pilfered some of the equipment that he bought for a project. It was normally stored in the receiving department until needed. The theft caused a delay in completion of the project and a cost overrun. Solution? Bob started having project equipment delivered to his office, storing it there. After a while, there were boxes filled with equipment stashed along every wall of his office. Admittedly, it looked like a junk heap!

One day, the Bell Park plant manager stopped in and told him to *"clean it up!"*

Bob overreacted, carried all the project equipment back to the receiving department, and cleaned off every surface in his office. There wasn't a scrap of paper anywhere.

"I'll show him! He wants it clean? Okay!"

It didn't work—the plant manager walked by, thought his office looked great, and complimented him on it. Grr!

Bob's old dentist had told him, *"You can say anything to anybody as long as you smile."*

Bob had found this to be wrong many times, and in this case, while chewing him out, Ralph Swenson had not been smiling! So overreacting following Ralph Swenson's loud lecture, Bob called the Houston Moore Products sales office and asked to see their manager for a job interview. Luckily, the office sales manager could not see him for two days because he was out of town. During that time, Bob had a chance to cool down. He knew that he really preferred engineering to sales. And his salary was higher than it had been at Moore Products.

As he was pondering his next step, Ralph Swenson appeared in the door.

Oh no, he thought, *I'm going to get dumped on again!*

But Ralph was there to apologize for his behavior. He said that he should not have treated Bob that way, yelling and carrying on. He made it clear that there was still proper procedure to be followed, but the issue should have been handled differently. He also indicated that his contacts at the Deer Park olefins plant had told him the new method for orifice calculations was saving time and money. They thanked Ralph for sending it to them! Ralph then told Bob that he was pleased with his performance. Wow! Bob cancelled the interview appointment with Moore Products. This was a lesson in managing—if you have to discipline an employee, first do it with grace, and then make sure you follow up by complimenting them on something in their performance.

Poor management was nothing new for Bob. When he was a first lieutenant in the army, he was stationed at Fort Dix, New Jersey, with the job of ammunition officer on the troop training ranges. He was always bothered by the fact that the folks needing the ammo had to drive out from the post to the ranges to get his signature—then drive completely back across the post to the ammunition dump to pick it up, then again drive back across the post to the ranges a second time for their training. So Bob prepared a staff study document explaining the problem, suggesting that they move him to the ammunition dump. That would save hundreds of trips per year across the post. After waiting two months, he asked Major "Moose" Miller, his direct boss, what had been the response. Moose told him that the colonel didn't want to make waves, and stuck the study in his desk drawer.

Being the stubborn person he was, Bob overreacted and submitted the exact same staff study under the Army Suggestion Program. Within one month, the colonel sent the Army Suggestion Program "suggestion" out to Bob for his comments. Duh! Bob replied that it was the best idea he had ever heard! Of course, it was, it was his idea! Long story short, they moved Bob to the ammunition dump, his idea got implemented, and the army started saving gasoline. This story had similarities to his present head office boss chewing him out for a good idea—Bob was more interested in achieving the objective than in following rigid protocols.

One disadvantage of being relocated to downtown Houston was that Bob didn't get to see Betty Marcum as much as he would like during the day. They had been on several dates, and their relationship seemed to be developing nicely. He gave her a call and asked if she could take time to come downtown for lunch at Treebeard's. They set up a date and time.

Bob had come to believe that Treebeard's Restaurant has the best carrot cake in the world. The name Treebeard's is a reference to the Spanish moss that hangs from the large cypress and oak trees along the bayous in Louisiana (Tree Beards). It reflects the fact that much of their menu originated in Louisiana, and the area is known for its friendly people as well as the flavorful food. The restaurant is located in the Houston downtown tunnel system—perhaps not the best ambiance. The tunnel system has multiple branches and snakes its way under most of the large Houston skyscrapers. It makes a convenient way to move around the city without having to deal with the traffic at ground level—and it is air-conditioned (very important in Houston).

Betty drove to Houston and parked in the lot across from Massey Tower, where Bob's office was located on the eleventh floor. She gave him a call, and he met her in the lobby. They went up to look at Bob's office, and although he said *an office is an office,* she was impressed with the view of the city. Then they took the elevator down to the lobby, and the escalator down to the tunnel level. It was a ten-minute walk to Treebeard's via the tunnels.

Betty remarked, *"It reminds me of an ant farm—with all the 'ants' crawling around looking for lunch."*

They arrived and were seated. As they looked at the menu, Bob recommended the seafood gumbo and the shrimp étouffée. He was saving his recommendation for carrot cake until later.

Betty went with Bob's recommendations and ordered the shrimp étouffée and a cup of seafood gumbo to start with. Since he had sent her in that direction, Bob ordered the same thing. He did warn her that after eating the shrimp étouffée, she would be tasting it the rest of the day. Treebeard's in the tunnels is only open for lunch, so they are quite efficient in getting the food to their customers quickly, and the gumbo arrived in a couple of minutes. One of the dangers of gumbo is that a chef may try to use spice to burn your tongue off. This gumbo was just right, not too spicy, and they spooned down the excellent seafood soup.

After telling Betty how nice she looked (always the salesman) and asking about her day, he asked her, *"Has there been any progress in your investigation of the fires and explosion at the olefins plant?"*

She said, *"There have been several people who said they recognized the person in the sketch, but none of those tips actually checked out. Our police forensic folks have not come up with any more evidence. But the hair discovered at the apartment complex is still out for DNA analysis."*

Bob said, *"That's not very encouraging. Are there any bright spots?"*

She said, *"Yes—per your suggestion, I have checked into anyone 'selling short' large amounts of Massey stock, and I've found one candidate. He is in Massey's upper management."*

Bob asked her who it was.

Betty would not tell Bob his name since there was no proof of illegal activity yet. She thanked Bob for the lead on short selling, and said she had an appointment with "Mr. X" the next day at 3:00 p.m. If in this meeting he looked suspicious, she would investigate his communications and financial transactions around the time of the fires and explosion to see if there was any connection. If the short sale was involved, she said she might alert the Securities and Exchange Commission of possible insider trading. But she would wait until after the interview to draw any conclusions.

They finished the excellent meal, and the waiter approached them to see if he could bring them dessert. Betty said no, but Bob became Treebeard's best salesman, strongly recommending their carrot cake, and she finally succumbed to his bad influence. She agreed that it was the best carrot cake she had ever eaten, but questioned Bob's statement that it was the best in the entire world. After all, there was much of the world she hadn't seen yet. They walked back to the Massey Building hand in hand before Betty had to leave for Deer Park. Without question, their relationship was becoming more serious.

Bob was not above doing some detective work on his own, and he planned to watch Betty arrive in the lobby the next day, determine the floor she went to, and see who "Mr. X" was.

CHAPTER 7

THE TUNNELS AND
THE CHASE

Bob got up an hour earlier than normal the next morning and drove to work without eating breakfast. On the way out of the apartment complex, he thought he noticed a white SUV following him. But within a couple of blocks, he lost sight of it, and assumed he was overreacting. The traffic was much lighter than he was used to, and he thought he might go in early every morning if his boss would let him work flexible hours.

He reached the parking garage about ninety minutes earlier than normal and decided to explore the tunnels below Massey Tower. The Houston tunnel system is a network of subterranean, climate-controlled, pedestrian walkways that link ninety-five full city blocks, twenty feet below Houston's downtown streets. It is approximately six miles long and has many restaurants and shops. In the tunnel below Massey Tower, he found "gourmet" breakfast dining at McDonald's, and decided on their Egg McMuffin with coffee. Well, maybe not gourmet, but still delicious.

After breakfast, he went up to the lobby of Massey Tower to scout out a position where Betty Marcum would not notice him. He remembered that Betty's appointment with "Mr. X" was at 3:00 p.m., but had no idea who Mr. X was or which floor his office was on. There was a small branch of Chase Bank on one side of the lobby. Looking in, he noticed a stand-up desk in the middle of the bank where folks could make out deposit or withdrawal slips. There was a full view of the lobby from that position, and he would be able to see all people coming in and out of the area to use the elevators. Most people with a mission in the office building would not notice someone in the middle of the bank. He could also see all of the elevator banks, which luckily had dials above each elevator indicating which floor it was on. There were three elevator banks to cover the thirty floors. Head office Engineering was located on three floors—floors 11 through 14 (there was no thirteenth floor—architects were apparently still superstitious), but he doubted that Mr. X was an engineer. Anyway, problem 1 was solved for the amateur detective!

It was still an hour before Bob's normal start time, so he again entered the tunnels to do some exploring. Without a map, it is quite easy to get lost in the tunnel system. This had happened to Bob before, and when that happened, he found the best solution was to go up to ground level in whatever building he found himself, go outside, and read the street signs. On the way down the escalator, he glanced upward and thought he saw someone duck out of the way.

He thought, *After that attack at my apartment, I'm becoming paranoid.*

He decided to explore and find out if he could find his way to the Alley Theatre. It is the oldest professional theater company in Texas and the third oldest resident theater in the United States. He planned to invite Betty to an upcoming performance of *Our Town*. He knew that he needed to go through Pennzoil Place, and remembered where the Pennzoil tunnel went off to the right. He decided to run a little experiment. He rushed to the Pennzoil tunnel, turned right, and looked for a place to hide where he could see the previous tunnel. Sure enough, within thirty seconds, a man limped by, continuing on in the previous tunnel. Today, the Tin Man was dressed in a suit and tie, and he was clean-shaven except for a mustache. Bob quickly snapped a picture of the man, side view, with his cell phone camera. The tunnels were beginning to fill with people, so Bob didn't think he needed to be concerned about an attack; and the Tin Man had lost him for the time being.

The tunnel ran into a tee under the Pennzoil building, and Bob turned left. After several crazy turns, this branch came into the Bank of America building, where it made a right angle passing over to Jones

Plaza, which is across the street from Jones Hall. The Jesse H. Jones Hall for the Performing Arts is a performance venue and the permanent home of the Houston Symphony Orchestra and Society for the Performing Arts. Heading toward Jones Hall, he came to another tee in the tunnel, turned left, and in about fifty yards came to the Alley Theatre. Success!

I should have left a trail of bread-crumbs, he thought. Since he didn't want to be late for work, he found his way up to ground level, recognized Louisiana Street, and headed back for Massey Tower at street level. He was at his desk in fifteen minutes, reviewing some instrument specifications for a new isoprene unit for the Bell Park, Ohio, plant.

Bob went to lunch at James Coney Island with a few of the head office instrument engineers. He kept glancing around trying to spot any unusual activity. This was difficult, since the streets were jammed with the lunch crowd. The guys wanted to hear about Bob's run-in with the knife-wielding villain. He related the events of the attack, laughed it off, and noted to himself that it didn't seem quite so frightening at twelve noon in a crowd of people. He did not let on that he had seen the culprit that same morning.

It was difficult to keep his mind on his work after lunch. A couple of times he had to repeat reviewing something because his mind wandered to the upcoming "surveillance case." At 2:45 p.m., he headed down to the Massey Tower lobby. Confirming that Betty was not in the lobby early, he went into the Chase Bank and tried to make himself inconspicuous by fiddling with the deposit slips. The bank guard gave him a cursory glance, but decided the nicely dressed businessman was no threat. Bob discovered how hard it is to play around "doing nothing" for fifteen minutes. But his wait was rewarded. Betty entered the lobby at five minutes to 3:00 p.m., looked at the elevator banks to determine which one she wanted, and selected the one that covered floors 21 to 30. Bob had been right. Mr. X was not a lowly engineer, he was in upper management—they always locate on the highest floors. He wondered if the planes that hit the New York Trade Center buildings on the top floors would change that. Unfortunately, two other people entered the elevator with Betty. Uh-oh!

Bob watched the elevator dial as it began rotating clockwise as soon as the twenty-first floor was reached. Where would it stop? Within seconds, the dial stopped at 29, then after a few seconds moved to 30. Mr. X was located on one of these two floors. As soon as the dial showed the elevator descending, Bob got into the next elevator available and pushed 29. It seemed like it took forever to reach the twenty-ninth floor, but he got a break—the doors opened, and he was immediately in a reception room. Betty was nowhere to be seen, so he quickly ducked back in the elevator and pushed 30. There was another reception area on 30, but Bob glanced to his left and saw Betty walking down the long hallway. He watched as she entered the last door on the right. Bob followed her path until he got to that door and read the title, *"John Swisher—Vice President of Operations."*

Unknown to Bob, the Tin Man recognized that he had lost his quarry when he went by the Pennzoil tunnel. He made an attempt to follow him down that tunnel, but after running into several possible turns, he gave up and decided to wait in the lobby of Massey Tower. He followed Bob as he had lunch at James Coney Island and returned to his office. He found a small alcove that had marble benches and sat watching the lobby from there. Knowing that the parking garage was accessed from another elevator bank, he was sure that he would not miss his quarry.

At 2:45 p.m., he noticed Bob come down and enter the Chase Bank. He could not figure out what he was doing, spending ten minutes at the stand-up desk, while never going to the teller counters. His patience was rewarded. He saw Lieutenant Betty Marcum enter the lobby and go into an elevator. His quarry watched carefully, then entered the same elevator bank. The only witness that might be able to identify him with the fires and explosion was on his way to the top of the building. He would wait for his return, and then deal with him.

Bob had achieved his objective: Mr. X was Massey's vice president of operations—John Swisher. He was the one who had benefitted from the short sale of Massey stock. Bob took the elevator back to the lobby. He had no idea that the Tin Man was observing his every move. Bob switched elevator banks and went to his office on the eleventh floor. The Tin Man noted the floor on which his quarry worked. Perhaps he would make a visit later if his plan today should fail.

Bob was unable to concentrate on his project and kept going over the day's crazy happenings. There was no danger of him changing careers to become a private detective—the pressure put his stomach in knots all day. He did an Internet search on John Swisher and found that he had worked his way up through the ranks at Massey. He spent three years as a process engineer in the monomer unit at the Norco, Louisiana, plant. He was then promoted to operations manager at the same plant and, after another five years, was made plant manager at the Los Angeles chemical plant. He was transferred to his present position two years ago. This type of individual was referred to as a "blue flamer," which usually meant that the person had a "sponsor" in upper management who ensured they progressed up through the ranks quickly. Swisher was now manager over all of Massey's operations in the United States. Betty had told Bob that he had "short sold" a large quantity of stock just prior to the fires and explosion at Deer Park. Mighty suspicious!

Around 4:30 p.m., Betty called Bob and asked if she could take him to dinner since she was in downtown Houston for a meeting with the Houston Police Department.

He readily agreed and asked, *"How did your meeting with John Swisher go?"*

The telephone seemed to go dead.

Betty said, *"How did you know about John Swisher?"*

Bob told her he was omniscient, and promised to tell her over dinner. She suggested Treebeard's, but Bob reminded her that they were only open for lunch. He suggested Brennan's on Smith Street. Brennan's has a New Orleans character and cuisine, specializing in turtle soup, oysters, and more. Betty agreed to meet him there at 5:30 p.m.

It seemed like when Bob left his office at 5:00 p.m. to pick up his car, everyone in Houston was leaving at the same time. The Tin Man had located Bob's car, but decided there were too many people around to make another attempt on his life in the parking garage. His car was parked one level up, so he followed Bob's car to the checkout booth. Since Bob had a parking authorization pass, he breezed on through in no time. The Tin Man had to stop, have his parking ticket read, and pay. He threw a $20 bill at the attendant and gunned his car out into Walker Street. He glanced to his right just in time to see his quarry a block ahead, turning left onto Smith Street. Fortunately, the lights were with him, and he was soon only a car length behind.

It was twenty-three blocks from where Bob turned onto Smith Street to Brennan's Restaurant. He was driving his old beat-up Jeep Cherokee and glanced in his rearview mirror, noticing the white SUV that appeared to be following him. He wondered if it was the same SUV that he had noticed at the apartment complex that morning. The lights on Smith Street were timed to allow traffic to flow smoothly at around 35 mph, but the white SUV was running both yellow and red lights to keep up. Bob decided to run a test. When he got stopped at the next red light, the SUV was two cars behind him, one lane to his right. He checked for cross traffic and gunned his Jeep through the red light. The white SUV drove over on the right sidewalk and also ran the light. Proof positive—Bob was in trouble!

The Tin Man opened his glove compartment and pulled out a Glock 9 mm semiautomatic pistol. He realized he had been discovered and raced to catch up with the Jeep. His plan was to pull alongside and shoot Bob through the window. This should be easy since his SUV had a new 400 hp engine. With about fifteen blocks remaining to Brennan's, this began looking like a video game. Slow down when a red light was in the path, check for cross traffic, and accelerate through the intersection—then repeat. What Bob did not notice was that the two cars racing down Smith Street had picked up a third car. Lieutenant Betty Marcum had left earlier than Bob and had parked along the right side of Smith Street waiting for Bob's Jeep to go by. When Bob and his "tail" ran the red light, she pulled out and started following, also running lights where necessary.

Two blocks before Brennan's, the white SUV gunned the engine and pulled even with the left side of Bob's Jeep. The Tin Man had his right-side window down and raised his Glock to fire. What he didn't notice immediately was the car right behind him with the flashing lights. Betty Marcum had seen him raise his weapon, turned on the flashing beacon she carried on her dashboard, leaned out the driver's side window, and fired three shots through the rear window of the SUV with her left hand. This caused the Tin Man to fire his Glock wide, missing Bob's Jeep completely. He hit the gas, accelerated down Smith Street, continuing on where it merged with Milam Street, and zoomed onto the Southwest Freeway entrance.

*　　*　　*

Bob and Betty pulled over to the right side of the road, and Betty ran up to see if Bob was okay. He was upset, but had no injuries.

He said, *"I've got a gun in my glove compartment. What the heck was I thinking?"*

Then he surprised Betty by asking, *"Are you still up for dinner? I'm hungry!"*

After calling in an APB (all-points bulletin) on the white SUV, she agreed.

Brennan's was in the next block, so they both pulled into the parking lot and went inside. When making reservations, Bob had asked for a table against the wall looking at the entrance. He remembered Betty's preference, and tonight he recognized the wisdom of that choice. However, they were not disturbed during the meal.

Seconds after they were seated, Betty demanded, *"How did you know I visited John Swisher this afternoon?"*

Bob said, *"You aren't the only detective at this table. I followed you! I'm considering leaving engineering to become a private detective!"*

Betty found this less than humorous and warned him that it was now obvious he was in danger. Bob thanked her for saving his life and assured her that his detective career was coming to an end.

He congratulated her on taking out the culprit's rear window using her left hand. She said that it was standard for her to use her left hand part-time at the gun range to handle times like this. Bob planned to add that to his firing routine. Betty had identified the Tin Man's vehicle as a new Ford Explorer ST and memorized the culprit's license plate during the chase; it later turned out the plate had been stolen off an eighty-five-year-old woman's Volkswagen Jetta—she had not noticed it was missing. An eighty-five-year-old woman was a pretty unlikely candidate for a high-speed gun battle, and even less likely as the chemical plant arsonist.

Bob related his sighting of the Tin Man that morning in the tunnels (leaving out the best part for last). Betty said she wouldn't let him out of her sight from now on. Although Betty had put out an APB on a white Ford Explorer SUV, there were probably ten thousand white Ford Explorers in Houston. In different areas of the country, an APB is known as a BOLO (be on the lookout).

Bob suggested, *"You might want to check repair shops for rear-window replacements. You put several holes in that guy's window."*

Betty said, *"That is already being done, and the Houston Police Department is cooperating in the search. Tomorrow morning, detectives will be interviewing people in the Massey Tower, the tunnel system, and the Massey Parking Garage, to see if anyone saw the suspect and could identify him.*" Based on Bob's contact with Tin Man in the tunnels, she called and expanded the interviews to the tunnel teeing off to Pennzoil Place. But Bob had left out a pleasant surprise—he showed her his cell phone side view photo of the Tin Man, and said it might help people remember if they had seen him.

* * *

Betty said, *"And you waited until now to tell me!?"*

Bob said, *"I always save the best for last!"*

The iPhone photo was slightly blurry since Tin Man had been walking at the time, but Betty thought she could get her forensic folks to clear it up. She would then add it to the APB/BOLO and place copies on the Massey plant bulletin boards.

Just then, the waiter approached their table to take their orders.

CHAPTER 8

TWO MEALS AND A PLANT CHECK

Brennan's was crowded and a bit noisy, and since they had not yet looked at the menus, they asked the waiter to come back later. Bob selected the snapping turtle soup to start with, and Betty chose the seafood gumbo, wanting to compare it to Treebeard's gumbo. Bob's warning about spicy gumbo went unheeded. Bob ordered the blue crab stuffed snapper with sides of sorghum-glazed brussels sprouts and crawfish andouille mac and cheese. Betty chose the gulf fish Pontchartrain, with garden vegetables and pecan haricot vert and wax beans. Obviously, the car chase had not ruined their appetites.

While the meals were being prepared, Bob asked Betty, *"What did you learn when you interviewed John Swisher?"*

She indicated, *"He denied any wrongdoing regarding the 'short sale' of Massey stock, insisting that he had no 'insider information,' but that the oil industry was in for a bad period, and that he had decided to bet on that. I then asked if he knew anything about the fires and the explosion at Deer Park."*

He insisted, *"It was just bad luck. After all, chemical plants are dangerous places."* He also commented, *"I have enough money that I can afford to take risks like short selling, but I would never take risks with people's lives."*

Betty remarked, *"He is a good salesperson, but I came away feeling that he wasn't telling me all the truth."*

Bob suggested that she "follow the money" and see what shape Swisher's finances were really in. Betty said that, with a search warrant, she was already looking for any large expenditures that he had made, and they were reviewing his phone communications to see if there were any anomalies. If they ever identified the Tin Man, this would be important for identifying a connection between them. In fact, if there were many calls to an unknown individual prior to the times of the fires and explosion, it could be a major clue.

Their appetizers arrived, and they dug in. Both of them were surprised at how the chase and shooting had actually increased their appetites. Betty commented that Bob seemed quite calm after being shot at, and he told her that he had been a first lieutenant in the army (kidding her that she wasn't the only lieutenant at the table). He said he had fortunately not been in any battle zones but had been exposed to live fire while at Fort Dix, New Jersey. He indicated that he had been the ammunition officer at Fort Dix, responsible for supplying ammunition to all of the ranges (pistol, rifle, grenade, 105 Howitzer, etc.).

When the weather was dry, the live fire on the ranges often set off brush fires. Range headquarters had a fire engine that normally handled the fires without outside help, but Bob was sometimes asked to coordinate the firefighting. He recalled one fire that was moving fast because of higher-than-normal winds. The ranges had firebreaks, where the brush was cleared down to the dirt. The principle was simple—the fire would come up to the firebreak and die out due to lack of fuel. Also, the roads running through the ranges acted as firebreaks. This particular fire was different in that its direction was heading off of Fort Dix, and had a children's orphanage in its path. Talk about the potential for bad press! As was typical, the range officers had the troops who were being trained pulled off of the ranges to help fight the fire. Bob said he was supervising the effort and told a second lieutenant to have his troops line up along a firebreak road that ran along the border of Fort Dix. They were to face away from the fire and to stamp out any sparks that carried across the road. This was a fairly typical strategy.

But the second lieutenant panicked and shouted, *"You are going to burn all these men to death!"*

Bob said that he got up in his face and shouted some words he never used in Sunday school, telling him that if he didn't calm down and lead his men, he would personally see that he got to see a court-martial up close and personal.

The second lieutenant calmed down, got his men organized; the fire came up to the firebreak and died out just as expected. Later, Bob discussed the event with another range officer, and discovered that the second lieutenant had fought fires in California, where the flames literally leaped through trees and underbrush. His past experiences caused him to panic over this brush fire because he expected it to behave the same way. Admittedly, watching a brush fire come toward you was frightening—this was why they had the troops face away from the fire, but Bob had seen this strategy work many times, and it was successful this time in protecting the orphanage.

Betty changed the subject to weapons.

Bob said, *"I go to a local range weekly to keep my pistol skills up-to-date."*

Betty asked, *"What weapons do you own?"*

Bob said, *"I have a shotgun, an old pump-action .22 rifle, an AR15, a small Ruger 9 mm pistol, and two Sig Sauer 9 mm pistols. I prefer the Sig Sauer pistols over the Ruger, but they are harder to conceal, so I generally take the Ruger when I carry. And I almost forgot, I just purchased a Sig Sauer P938, 9 mm pistol, which is about the same size as the Ruger. I'm looking forward to testing it when it arrives. My latest fad has been installing laser sights on a couple of the weapons. It has really improved my accuracy."*

Betty said, *"I see that you are gun crazy. I pretty much limit myself to my service weapon, but I practice frequently at the police gun range."*

Bob said, *"I'm not gun crazy—I'm just crazy! We need to meet at my gun range, and you can give me some pointers on left-hand firing."*

Betty said that was a great idea.

Both enjoyed their dinners, but Betty said her gumbo was too hot. Bob felt she had one "I told you so" coming—and she accepted it graciously. For dessert, Bob had Southern pecan pie with vanilla ice cream. It was unusual in that it had chocolate and caramel in it. Very tasty! Betty settled on the creole bread pudding crowned with berries and pecans. It was so big she took some home in a to-go box. Even though Betty had invited him to dinner, Bob paid the bill, and they cautiously walked to their vehicles.

*   *   *

On the drive home, Betty insisted on following Bob all the way to his apartment complex. She escorted him to the door, checked out the apartment, and thanked him for an interesting (although dangerous) date. He assured her that he would begin carrying his new P938 for defense when it arrived. Texas allows concealed handguns, and Bob had a license to carry. He felt sympathy for those living in states that did not allow you to defend yourself. He thought it might be time to risk kissing Betty for the first time. She did not resist, and their relationship took another step forward. They agreed to meet for breakfast at Denny's on the Pasadena Freeway (225) early the next morning. Betty again arranged for a patrol car to check Bob's apartment complex a few times during the night. Apparently, the Tin Man was regrouping; there were no additional incidents.

The menu at Denny's had always intrigued Bob. He selected the time-proven standard—the Grand Slam. The grand slam in baseball is when a batter hits a home run with the bases loaded—four runs. Denny's Grand Slam consisted of four "runs"—pancakes, eggs, sausage links, and bacon strips. Bob planned to clear the bases! Betty ordered Moons Over My Hammy (ham and eggs in a sandwich). As usual, Denny's coffee was outstanding.

Bob asked Betty what her plans were for the day.

She indicated, *"I will be following up with our investigating team to see if there have been any worthwhile leads."*

Bob told her, *"I will be going to the olefins unit in Deer Park to see how the plant rebuild is going. I also want to determine how difficult it would be to get into the plant without going through security. Most of the plant is surrounded with chain-link fencing, and to most people, these fences seem unclimbable. But I did some reading last night before going to bed. I just happened to read a* New York Times Magazine *article titled, 'How to Climb a Chain-Link Fence,' of all things. And yes, there was actually an article covering that subject! It must have been a slow month for the editor.*

"The article indicated that our minds have been trained to think of a fence as a barrier. Part of going over the top of one requires a psychological shift. You have to believe you can make it over. The author of the article was a woman who runs women's survival boot camps. She also said, 'It's not uncommon for trainees to run up to the fence and just stop. To build the confidence to go over, you must think of yourself as a creature that cannot be contained so easily.' The article then showed the technique for getting over

the fence. I plan to give it a try, as well as look for evidence that anyone else had used the fence as a method of entry."

Betty again warned him that he was not a trained investigator, to which he gave his standard reply: *"Not to worry!"*

*   *   *

When Bob arrived at the start-up trailer, he stopped in to see his old boss, Jack Fishbane, to let him know he was there to see how the rebuild was going. As usual, Jack had everything organized down to the last detail, and showed Bob the schedule they were on. It looked like they would be ready to check the instrumentation out in three weeks, with a start-up planned in four weeks. This was good news for Bob since he was getting bored with his make-work job at head office. And he was ready to stop commuting downtown for a while. He asked Jack if it was okay for him to take a look at the work going on. Jack said it was fine.

Before going to the field, Bob stopped at each office and said howdy to each of the start-up team members. He pulled their chain, telling them they were taking too long—and to get on the stick. In jest, he asked if there had been any more fires or explosions. Everyone took it in the humorous way it was intended. Fred Conway said he wasn't in any hurry—with the plant down, he hadn't had any boiler trips.

Jack Fishbane told Bob, *"Get your butt out of here, and stop wasting my folks' time."*

Although this was meant in fun, he headed for the field.

As he walked down under the main pipe rack to the control room, Bob couldn't help remembering the time when he saw the person, now referred to as the Tin Man, sneaking in and out of the motor control center. He passed the boiler feedwater pump that had its motor contactor jammed, causing the electrical fire. When he got to the control room, he noticed that the old sketch of the Tin Man was still on the bulletin board. Someone had drawn a handlebar mustache on it. Except for the "handlebar part," the mustache made it a pretty good likeness. It would soon be joined by a side view photograph of the Tin Man walking in the Houston tunnels.

CHAPTER 9

REPAIRS, SECURITY ISSUES, AND ROBBERY

Bob decided to walk through the gasoline hydrotreater (GHT) first, since it had been the last fire, then check the control room electrical fire area, the hydrogen flange fire area, and lastly the compressor fire area. Repairs to the GHT heater were close to completion. The I beam supports for the heater had to be replaced since the heater was tilted twenty degrees following the fire. They were fortunate that the heater had not toppled over. New heater tubes had been received to replace the tubes damaged by flame impingement. They had been welded in place, and were being pressure tested. Scaffolding was in place for the painters to "make the heater pretty" by painting over the burned spots. They had followed Bob's schedule regarding GHT instrumentation and control repairs. Damaged instrumentation had been replaced, wiring and tubing checked out, and it would be ready for final start-up testing in a couple of weeks. The progress was remarkable.

As expected, the control room fire area looked great. It had been repaired prior to the latest two fires. The hydrogen flange fire damage was completely repaired and ready for start-up.

But the fire damage caused by the three-inch block valve being left open was the most extensive. The junction boxes had been placed, and tubing and wiring were being terminated in these boxes. The cabling between the boxes was to be delivered this week. Cable trays had been repaired or replaced. It would take about two weeks to run the new cable and terminate all of the tubes and wires. Then it would have to be thoroughly tested. This area seemed to be on the critical path for start-up. Everything would have to go just right to meet Jack Fishbane's estimate of four weeks to start-up. But if anyone could make it happen, it was Jack.

In the control room, the sketch of the Tin Man had been replaced (with drawn-in mustache removed), and an eight-by-ten-inch photo of the Tin Man in the Houston tunnel had been placed alongside it. Although the Deer Park Police Forensic Department had improved the photo, it was still slightly blurry.

Bob thought, *Next time, I'll ask the Tin Man to pose for the picture!*

Regardless, folks should be able to identify the man from the two documents.

Bob then decided to walk the perimeter of the plant, looking for any place someone might have entered undetected. As expected, the plant was surrounded by chain-linked fencing. He was armed with his newfound knowledge from the *New York Times Magazine* article titled "How to Climb a Chain-Link Fence." As he walked along the inside of the east fence, built close to the chemical plant entrance road, he was surprised to see a number of spots where the fence passed close to some object that would make entry easier. For example, it passed under power wiring that had one of its telephone pole supports close enough to aid someone trying to gain access. Indeed, in this spot it seemed like the top of the chain-link fence had several of its links bent over where someone may have stepped, causing the damage. He would mention it to Betty the next time he saw her.

In the north section, the soil under the fence had been eroded away by flash flooding. The average-sized man could easily crawl under the fence for access. He found one more security problem on the west side. When the fence was built, a nearby tree must have been quite small— no more—it was about a foot in diameter, and a couple of its lower branches extended over the fence. It would not take Houdini to use that tree for an entrance point. Add to that the *New York Times* article indicating that anyone in good shape could easily climb a chain-link fence. Bob considered trying the method to climb it himself. However, it seemed like there were easier ways of entrance than taking the "jump and climb method." Summarizing this in his mind, Bob thought that the plant security stunk (to use the technical term) for limiting entrance by someone bent on destruction.

Entrance, of course, left the perpetrator with the opposite problem—how to get out without being detected. The objects helping him to get in would not necessarily help him to get out. The "muscle man approach" of climbing the fence would work, but that method seemed a bit extreme at this point, and the Tin Man had a bad limp, so jumping and climbing seemed unlikely. Bob decided to watch the plant security gate during shift change. Inside the main gate was a building that housed time card machines. As people reported to work, and left by the same gate, they entered this building and ran their time card through machines that recorded their entrance and exit times.

He noticed that the one guard on duty was not paying much attention to the folks checking out, except to make sure they were not carrying company property out the gate. He remembered the old joke about the guard who could not figure out what this employee was taking out in his wheelbarrow each night since he inspected it every time he left. The punch line—he was stealing wheelbarrows. In the Massey guard's case, he might have caught someone stealing a wheelbarrow, but would probably not notice anything else out of the normal. There were no security cameras—another security flaw.

The guard seemed to be much more interested in making sure no one got in without having a Massey badge. Shift change resembled a Chinese fire drill—mass confusion—although everyone seemed to know what was expected of them. The sequence was for the next shift to check in first, report to their job for duty, relieve the person on the earlier shift, and then that person would check out for the day. Multiply that by one hundred, and you get the flavor for the potential confusion. Bob visualized the Tin Man, dressed pretty much like all the other workers, getting in line to check out. He would have taken a punch card with him, run it through the time machine, and headed out the gate without so much as a challenge.

Bob planned to get with the plant safety manager to discuss the security issues he had discovered, but then he thought, *He'll be upset that some instrument guy is telling him how to run his business.*

So he decided to wait and tell Betty—the information coming from a police detective would carry more weight. They were going to meet at the local bowling alley that evening—that would be a good time to discuss it.

Bob returned to the start-up trailer to let Jack Fishbane know what he had found, and let him know he was leaving. Since it was close to 4:00 p.m.—he had been working long hours, and at this time of day, it would take him forty-five minutes to drive downtown—he decided to knock off for the day. He got in the Jeep and drove over to his Deer Park apartment. He climbed the outside stairs to his second-floor apartment and then noticed that his apartment door was open slightly.

He immediately ran down back down the steps and got his new 9 mm Sig Sauer pistol from the Jeep glove compartment. When he got back to the second floor, he approached his door cautiously with the gun ready in firing position. He threw the door wide open and stepped inside and to the left to prevent his silhouette from being in the doorway. No one was in the living room area, but the place had been trashed. He quickly checked the bedroom and bathroom—no one was there. Above the fireplace, a message was scrawled in permanent marker ink, *KEEP QUIET, OR DIE!!!*

Life was sure becoming exciting lately!

After calling Police Lieutenant Betty Marcum, he tried to assess the damage. He made sure he did not touch anything in case there were fingerprints. His four-drawer cabinet had been broken into, and the files and papers thrown around the room. His Dell T3610 computer had been thrown off his desk and was dangling off some wires that were still connected. The twenty-four-inch computer monitor had met the same fate, and it was obvious that the screen had shattered. His HP printer had been smashed with something heavy. He was hoping that the computer still worked, but until he bought a new monitor, he was dead in the water (perhaps not the best analogy at this particular time). He was not too concerned about loss of file information since he had two external hard disks he used for backup quarterly, and the one in the apartment had escaped damage. He had backed up the computer just a couple of days ago. The second of these backup hard disks was kept in his Massey office downtown, in case a fire should destroy everything in the apartment.

Furniture had been tipped over, his bed mattress was thrown on the floor, and just about anything in the kitchen cabinets had been cleared out onto the floor. His TV was facedown on the floor. A bookcase had been tipped over, and the books scattered around the room. The apartment looked like it had just been through an earthquake. On the positive side, Bob always carried his iPhone, iPad, and MacBook in a computer bag—so he was thankful for that. Using a tissue, he checked his cookie jar—the cookies were still there! After all, there are priorities! Fortunately, he had renter's insurance, and he wanted a thirty-six-inch monitor anyway!

Betty Marcum and her team arrived about twenty minutes after Bob found the break-in.

After making sure that Bob hadn't touched anything, she remarked, *"You sure keep a messy apartment!"*

For some reason, he didn't find that as amusing as she had hoped.

He replied, *"That's real funny, but the death threat over the fireplace keeps me from laughing hysterically!"*

She asked him when he had left for work and when he had returned. Her team split up—most interviewing folks in the apartment complex, a few collecting forensic evidence. The new players were from the Robbery Detail.

When the confusion settled down a bit, Bob told Betty, *"I have a pleasant surprise for you. Take a look at this."*

He took her over to the mantle above the fireplace. This was one of the reasons he had selected this apartment complex, they had fireplaces. On the mantle was a strange-looking plant. Betty commented that it was one of the ugliest plants she had ever seen.

Bob corrected her, *"I'll bet in a minute you will think it is extremely beautiful! Look closely."*

Betty got up close—and saw a lens looking back at her.

A few months before the break-in, Bob had become interested in surveillance cameras. He had tried one brand that was so complex he needed to talk to their factory people (in the Philippines) to get it to work. But then he discovered cameras by Amcrest. They were so easy to set up, via his iPhone, that he had one working within minutes. They were clever devices that could be remotely positioned, and they could send an email with photo attachments when either movement or sound sensed an intruder. In addition, any event like this would turn on video recording, stored on a removable minidisc.

Betty said, *"You were right—that plant is beautiful!"*

Bob complained that he had only installed one in the living room area. He grabbed his MacBook, accessed his email account, and surely enough, there were emails with attachments. He removed the minidisc and downloaded it to the MacBook. Since the forensic people had finished with his desk, they set it upright, and they went through the video files and emails.

They first looked at the video attachments on the minidisc. The first video showed a man wearing a ski mask searching the apartment—and he limped as he moved around. He wore gloves, so there wasn't much chance of getting fingerprints. He didn't appear to know what he was looking for since he searched everywhere randomly. Bob had installed a programmable thermostat in the apartment to save money. Since he was usually at work during this time of day, it was set at eighty-five degrees Fahrenheit, pretty hot. In the second video, the burglar appeared to be frustrated and began to tear the place apart. It became apparent that he was sweating heavily, soaking his tee shirt.

In the last video file, he moved toward the fireplace, got out a permanent marker, removed his heavy ski mask, and stepped up on a stool to write the death threat above the fireplace. His face was captured frontally. Since videos are not the crispest pictures, they started looking at the high-resolution photos that the fireplace camera had also captured and sent to Bob via email. Most of the photos had duplicate information that they had seen on the videos. But the last email had two photos of the burglar, up close, without ski mask, facing the camera. The quality of the photos was excellent. If this was the Tin Man, as he appeared to be, they now had a high-definition picture of him.

The police team wrapped up their investigation around 7:30 p.m. Bob asked Betty if she was still up for some bowling.

She said, *"Every time we have a date, you get shot at, you have a high-speed chase through Houston, or your apartment gets ransacked. Are you sure you want to go bowling? With your luck, I might drop a bowling ball on your foot!"*

Bob said he would chance it. Betty wanted to help him clear up the mess in his apartment, but he said he would take care of it in the morning. So they headed for the bowling alley. Bob was a reasonably good bowler, usually in the 140 area. But Betty was superb; all three games were above 160. The best part was the tacos and french fries from the concession area.

As they sat enjoying the meal, as usual, the conversation turned toward the arson/explosion case. Betty hated to admit it, but they had made little progress. She had found out that John Swisher, who made the short sale of Massey stock, was out of town during each of the fires and explosion. Of course, that did not mean he could not have hired the arsonist. Bob had made Betty a copy of the video and photo files. In the morning, she planned on getting her best people to see if they could identify the robber, perhaps asking a friend, Jack Lentor, at the FBI for help using facial recognition. Betty had dated Jack Lentor for a short time a few years back, and they were still on friendly terms.

Bob brought Betty up to date regarding his trip to the plant.

He indicated, *"Even though the plant is surrounded by chain-link fence, there are multiple ways that an intruder could get into the plant by climbing over or going under the fence. And if someone gets in, due to poor shift change security, there would be no problem getting back out. I have written down my findings, so please review the information with the plant safety manager to point out the security weaknesses. I'm afraid that if a lowly instrument engineer brings these security flaws up, he will ignore them."*

Betty agreed to do so, and pointed out that if Bob was right about the plant starting up in a few weeks, they were time limited in arresting the Tin Man before he could cause more problems.

She commented, *"We sure don't want any more fires or explosions!"*

Again, Betty followed Bob back to his apartment, came up to check it for intruders, and kissed him good night. Bob didn't think he needed her babying him, but he didn't want to miss the kiss good night. Bob spent a few minutes clearing some of the mess the Tin Man had left, then he put his mattress back on the bed and hit the sack. He slept with his 9 mm pistol under his pillow.

CHAPTER 10

PROGRESS

Betty Marcum reported to work at 8:00 a.m. and went to ask her investigating team members if any progress had been made on the case. As expected, the forensic team found no fingerprints in the apartment other than Bob Garver's and Betty's.

One of them joked, *"Betty, did you burgle that apartment?"*

She answered, *"Yeah, I'm moonlighting as a burglar."*

They did find a few hairs near the fireplace where the culprit had removed his ski mask. There was no root material, which provides the most accurate source of DNA. However, using the rest of the hairs, they were running mitochondrial DNA tests. Mitochondrial DNA is passed almost exclusively from mother to offspring through the egg cell, whereas the other type of DNA, nuclear DNA, is inherited from both parents. Nuclear DNA is certainly the best evidence; however, mitochondrial DNA can also be used as evidence in most cases. One interesting area of weakness is that all brothers and sisters share identical mitochondrial DNA.

Betty humorously thought, *I sure hope the Tin Man doesn't have a brother or sister in the arson business too!*

Sgt. Joe Lighten had called the FBI for assistance with photo facial identification. They had not been very helpful; and after several phone transfers to people who couldn't or wouldn't help, he hung up. Betty told him she had a friend who worked in the Houston FBI Office on the Northwest Freeway. She said she would talk to him later about running the Tin Man's photo through their facial recognition program. What she didn't let on was that the FBI agent, Jack Lentor, had dated her for a few months two years ago. They finally called it off because their schedules always seemed to conflict, and neither saw a future for the relationship. He was one of the few men she had dated who was slightly taller than her 6'2" height. A man's height, or lack thereof, normally did not bother her, but it was nice to "look up" to a man. His bushy blond hair and blue eyes didn't hurt either. Jack still held a warm spot in her heart. Hopefully, he would agree to help her with the facial identification.

Betty asked Joe Lighten to take several eight-by-ten-inch copies of the facial photo over to the Massey Plant and put them on the various bulletin boards alongside the artist's sketch and the blurry side view taken in the Houston tunnel. She asked whether anyone had received more tips—they had not. The APB/BOLO on the white Ford Explorer SUV had not produced anything, even with the license plate included. Betty indicated that she would contact the Texas Department of Public Safety (DPS) to see if they would issue a CLEAR Alert.

A CLEAR Alert helps law enforcement agencies find adults who are missing, kidnapped, or abducted and in immediate danger of injury or death. This type of alert also aims to help locate potential suspects, which would be its use this time. There are six (6) types of alerts that the Texas DPS can issue (Amber, Silver, Blue, Endangered, Camo, and Clear); and they appear on large electronic signs along many of the Texas highways, usually bearing the license plate of the vehicle in question.

Betty also planned to check out Bob Garver's findings regarding the security (or nonsecurity) of the fence around the Massey plant. She had a meeting set up in the afternoon with the Massey Safety Department to discuss her findings. In addition, she would have her team double-check Bob's apartment complex for any witnesses to the break-in. It should be a full day.

"Hey, Jack, a voice out of the past! This is Betty Marcum—how are you doing?"

Betty didn't know what to expect since they had not talked for over two years. Jack Lentor was surprised by the phone call. Although they had parted on friendly terms, lack of contact had convinced him that time in his life was over.

"Hi, Betty, how have you been?"

They spent several minutes updating each other on events over the last couple of years. Jack was now happily married.

As the conversation started to lag, Jack asked her, *"What can I do for you, Betty?"*

"Well, Jack, I am investigating the fires and explosions at the Massey Chemical plant in Deer Park. We have an excellent lead on an individual— even have a photograph of him during a break-in—but we've been unable to identify him. Is there any chance you could do me a favor and run the photo through your facial recognition program?"

Jack hesitated because it was "not by the book." The book would indicate she should go through channels, but he recognized that route was fraught with delays and might even get refused due to heavy workloads. On the other hand, Betty and he had been close.

He said, *"Can you send me an electronic file of the photo?"*

"Sure—in fact, I will send you two frontal photos, a blurry side view, and three videos."

"Wow! Why didn't you just nab the guy while taking the shots?"

"Because the videos and photos were taken by a surveillance camera."

"Okay—I'll be looking for your email."

"I'm sending them to you right now, please let me know when and if you get an identity. And thanks a lot!"

Betty grabbed a quick lunch, then drove over to the Massey plant and followed the chain-link fence where it paralleled the outside roads. It didn't take long for her to reach the same conclusions that Bob Garver had reached. There were several spots where an intruder could easily get over or under the fence. Time was slipping by, and she had to hurry to get to her meeting in the Safety Department. She went to the main gate entrance and called her contact in the Safety Department for permission to enter. Since the Safety Office was close to the gate, she left her car in the parking lot and walked in through the check-in/ check-out building. There was no shift change in progress, so she would have to come back later to get a flavor for the mass confusion that Bob Garver had described.

Randy Michaels was the plant safety manager, and he walked Betty down to the conference room. There were several folks already there, including the plant manager, Lou Samuels. Apparently, Lou was interested in getting a status on the investigation. Betty started the discussion by relating her observations about the chain-link fence protecting the plant. She said that she had not yet completely gone around the plant, but that she had already found several spots where access could easily be gained from the outside. She covered those in detail, showing them pictures she had taken on her iPhone. Lou Samuels glared at Randy Michaels and asked him how that was possible. Randy hemmed and hawed a bit and told him that the deficiencies would be corrected. Betty had not made Randy her friend with this, but that was not her goal.

Lou Samuels asked Betty to give a status of her investigation. She tossed several copies of the Tin Man's photo out on the conference room table, explaining that the individual in the picture was probably the arsonist who had become known as the Tin Man. Lou Samuels smiled for the first time. He asked who the culprit really was. Betty had to explain that they did not yet know his identity. She listed the attacks on Bob Garver: the initial knife attack at his apartment complex, the murder attempt in downtown Houston, and the break-in of his apartment. She noted that the only connection appeared to be the fact that Bob was the only eyewitness that had seen the Tin Man inside the olefins plant at the motor control center, where the electrical fire was initiated. Where the photos would nail him for robbery, Bob Garver could pin him to the specific crime of arson.

She described the Smith Street auto chase, and the fact that the Tin Man had fired at Bob Garver, but missed due to the four shots Betty had fired through his rear window. She explained that they now knew the car he was driving and its license number but, so far, even with an APB/BOLO, had not been able to find it. She indicated that they had DNA evidence from the break-in at Bob Garver's apartment. Lou Samuels seemed pleased that they were making progress, but he asked when they would catch the b******. Betty closed the meeting by explaining that the FBI was running facial recognition on the photos she had placed on the table. Lou asked the safety manager to make sure the picture was on every bulletin board in the plant.

Since it was close to shift change, Betty walked back to the check-in/check-out building with Randy Michaels. She used the occasion to apologize for getting him in hot water, explaining that she never expected the plant manager to be in the meeting. She emphasized that it was important to eliminate these chain-link fence entry points—Randy agreed, accepted her apology, and said the security issues would be taken care of quickly.

Their next task was to observe the new crew coming in for shift change. Betty noted that the guard was closely checking the new shift coming in to make sure they had badges, and it was unlikely that a nonemployee could gain access. The guard may have been more alert than usual since the top security guy was watching. The badges were distinctive and would be difficult to reproduce. Twenty minutes later, the exiting crew personnel were already lining up, waiting for quitting time. Others soon joined them in the building, and it became quite crowded. Betty had to agree with Bob Garver; it looked like a Chinese fire drill—mass confusion.

A siren sounded, and the "herd of cattle" surged through the time clock lanes, locating their time cards, punching them, and reinserting them in the time card racks. Betty commented to Randy that it would be extremely easy for the arsonist to blend in with the crowd and leave the plant without detection. She noted that the guard had closely checked the new shift coming in for badges, but did not seem to be paying as much attention to the shift exiting. Randy pointed out that for the exiting employees, the guard's main function was to make sure they were not stealing company property.

Betty made the obvious comment that some security automation via badge scanners would help solve both the entry-and-exit problem. The automated system could also be used to log entry and exit times for use for personnel payment information. She also pointed out that the addition of security cameras would help to troubleshoot security issues. Randy said that he had suggested these changes, but the plant manager said that money was the problem.

Betty thought the automated timekeeping would pay for itself, and commented, *"If it had prevented the olefins plant fires and explosion, the money saved could have purchased the best system in the world a thousand times over."*

She noted, *"It would be real nice if we could go back over videos to see if the Tin Man made an appearance prior to the fires and explosion."*

Randy said he would use those arguments on the plant manager to see if they could *"close the barn door after the horse was stolen."*

Betty headed back to the office to see if there was any news—in this case, no news was bad news. She contacted the Texas Department of Public Safety (DPS), and they agreed to issue a CLEAR Alert for the white Ford Explorer. The FBI had not called regarding the facial recognition. It had been a long day—Betty headed home.

CHAPTER 11

HEAD OFFICE CONFRONTATION

Bob Garver went back to his normal routine at Massey's head office in downtown Houston. He and Betty were now dating about once a week, and their relationship was growing more serious.

Betty's friend, Jack Lentor, at the FBI, had agreed to run the facial recognition program on the Tin Man's photo. He called Betty and, after a bit of small talk, said, *"Betty, we have discovered that this guy is a known arsonist, Marcus Stalinbeck. He has a police record of setting fires going back to his thirties. He has spent short stints in a couple of prisons, but has had no long sentences because no one was ever killed or injured in his fires. He immigrated to the US from Russia when he was thirty-five, and was considered a good candidate because of his experience in the refining business. But wait until you hear this: He was employed by Gazprom Neft in their Moscow refinery. And better yet, he was one of their instrument engineers—just the experience needed for a chemical plant arsonist. No one in police circles was aware that he is in the Houston area.*

"By the way, I need to thank you—my boss gave me kudos for finding this out."

Betty replied, *"Jack, that is great news! It confirms that he is the one who probably set the Massey fires."*

Jack said, *"This guy is dangerous. If he was following someone, or threatening them, they need to watch their back!"*

Betty said, *"Yeah, he has already tried to attack the guy he was following twice."*

Jack said, *"If you ever need anything else, give me a call—I can use all the compliments from my boss I can get!"*

Betty said, *"I might just take you up on that. This is an interesting case. I'll keep you informed. Talk to you later."*

After the call, Betty revised the existing APB/BOLO to include the additional information. Little did she know, she would need Jack Lentor's help in the near future.

The Texas DPS CLEAR Alert turned up the white Ford Explorer SUV in Livingston, Texas, about a one and a half–hour drive northeast of Houston. It was parked in a Walmart parking lot, wiped clean of fingerprints, and had been pressure-washed and vacuumed to remove trace evidence. Forensics went over the inside with sticky tape, hoping to find something left behind. They found a few hairs wedged in the driver's side seat—apparently, Stalinbeck (alias the Tin Man) was losing his hair. DNA testing revealed them to be a match to the ones discovered in Bob's apartment following the break-in. This placed Stalinbeck in the SUV, tying him to the shooting on Smith Street in downtown Houston. But so far, there was no clue as to where the Tin Man was hiding, if he was still even in the Houston area.

* * *

This was the day for the monthly project status meeting of the instrument engineers. Based on his trip to the Deer Park plant, Bob Garver brought Ralph Swenson and the other engineers up to date regarding the olefins plant rebuild. This was followed by each engineer giving a status on the projects for which they were responsible. As Mark Simmons, an instrument engineer, was giving his project status, the door of the conference room flew open, slamming against the wall stops. Into the room walked a red-faced man, about 5'6" tall, in a brown tailored Brooks Brothers suit.

He yelled more than said, *"Which one of you jokers is Bob Garver?"*

Bob replied, *"That's me. What's the problem?"*

The red-faced man said, *"Just who the h*** do you think you are, sending the police to my office to question me?!"*

Bob said, *"First of all, I don't send the police anywhere. And secondly, who the heck are you?"*

"I'm the vice president of operations for Massey Chemical Company, you jerk! And the police think I have been behind the fires and explosion at Deer Park."

Bob was not going to roll over for this turkey. He said, *"Well, are you? And do you have a name?"*

This did not sit well, and he said, *"I'm John Swisher, and your career is approaching its end."*

At this point, Ralph Swenson, Bob's boss, had enough. He stood up, slapped both hands on the table, and said, *"I don't care who you think you are, you can't come into my meeting and make accusations. Secondly, don't you threaten my engineers! Get your butt out of here before I sic these young engineers on you—and they'll teach you some manners the hard way!"*

Swisher mumbled something about *"We'll see about that."* and turned tail and left the meeting slamming the door behind him.

Ralph said, *"What the heck have you gotten yourself into now, Garver!"*

Bob replied, *"I've never met the man before today. Me? Sending the police? Give me a break, Ralph!"*

Ralph said, *"Let's finish the status meeting, and we'll talk about it in my office."*

As the engineers left the meeting, Mark Simmons joked, *"That was the most interesting status meeting I have ever been in! They're usually pretty boring."*

Bob replied, *"You ain't seen nothin' yet! Next month I'm planning a sing-along."*

Bob and Ralph Swenson proceeded down the hall to Ralph's office. Ralph started by saying, *"That was the VP of Operations! How did you manage to tick him off that much?"* Bob decided to bring Ralph up to date with what he knew regarding the investigation. He first told Ralph that he was dating the police lieutenant responsible for the investigation, and therefore was privy to some information about the case. He reminded Ralph that he had told him about seeing the Tin Man entering and leaving the motor control center just prior to the first fire. He then related how the arsonist attempted to knife him at his apartment complex—and Ralph remembered both incidents.

Bob then theorized that it was because he was the only eyewitness that could place the Tin Man in the olefins plant at the time of the first fire. Bob then told about being followed in the Houston tunnels and his sighting of the Tin Man. He showed him the photo that he had taken and given to the police. He then went over the car chase down Smith Street, where another attempt was made on his life, and the police shot out the rear window of Tin Man's SUV.

He told Ralph about the break-in in his apartment, and the fact that his surveillance camera had taken videos and photos of the Tin Man that had been turned over to the police. He showed Ralph one of the photos. He informed him that, as a result of an APB/BOLO, the police had found the SUV in Livingston and discovered inside some DNA evidence that matched other DNA evidence from the apartment break-in. With all that evidence, they now knew the identification of the arsonist—Marcus Stalinbeck, and the police and FBI were doing their best to find him.

Ralph Swenson had trouble believing that all this had been going on without him knowing about it. But he couldn't deny the photographs of the Tin Man.

He asked, *"How did John Swisher get involved in this?"*

Bob said that in discussing with Lieutenant Betty Marcum, his new beau, various avenues the investigation might follow, he had suggested that she see if anyone had used short selling of Marcum stock to make lots of money. She did that and found that John Swisher had made a bundle using that strategy.

"She must have mentioned me when she interviewed him," Bob said. *"That VP threatened to end my career, Ralph! Can he do that?"*

Ralph said, *"Over my dead body! Let's see if Lou Docker, the manager of Engineering, has time to talk with us."*

And down the hall they went. Lou Docker's secretary checked his schedule, buzzed him on the intercom, and got the okay for Ralph and Bob to go in.

Ralph started the conversation by saying, *"That pain in the butt, Swisher, stomped into my status meeting and threatened to get one of my engineers fired. We need to bring you up to speed on something so that you don't get blindsided."*

Lou said, *"Okay—go for it."*

Ralph then turned the meeting over to Bob Garver, who essentially repeated the entire story for Lou Docker's consideration. By the end, Lou was on the edge of his seat.

He commented, *"Ralph, you didn't tell me you had hired Thomas Magnum, PI! Holy cow, I had no idea all this was going on—a gunfight on Smith Street? I'm surprised I didn't see it in the paper. And one of our engineers, attacked three times? How did all this get kept secret?"*

Ralph said, *"I learned most of this from Bob today. Because Bob is dating the police investigating officer, he has access to some inside information—so keep most of this under your hat. But apparently, Swisher has been selling Massey stock short just prior to the fires and explosion, and following the fires and explosion, he made a pile of money cashing in on the stock price drop. That doesn't necessarily make him guilty of causing the arson and explosions, but it certainly looks suspicious. But, Lou, my concern today is whether he has the clout to get Bob canned."*

Lou said, *"From what you have told me, he has no basis for requesting Bob's termination. It is the police that are investigating him, not Bob. I've known John Swisher for over thirty years. He has always gone off half-cocked. I will call around and make sure folks know about his ranting and raving in your meeting. I don't think you will hear any more about this."*

Ralph stood up and headed for the door. *"Thanks, Lou, I just wanted to make sure you were prepared in case the brown stuff hit the fan."*

Lou said, *"Bob, don't worry about this, I will take care of it."*

On the way back to the engineers' offices, Ralph said, *"That's a good lesson for you. Always keep your boss informed of any problems that might develop—before they develop."*

Bob filed that away in his bag of tricks. Bob then told Ralph that he planned to tell Lt. Betty Marcum what had happened. Ralph didn't see any problem with that, although he noted that it might have the police interviewing Swisher again.

But then he said, *"Good—he'll see that we can't be bullied!"*

Once back in his office, Bob called Betty and asked to meet her for lunch. He suggested the Shrimp Galore on Telephone Road, just off the South Loop. It was about halfway between their work locations. He told her that they have great fried shrimp baskets. She looked its location up on the Internet and agreed to meet him at 1:00 p.m.

CHAPTER 12

THE HIT AND THE PROPOSAL

At 12:45 p.m., Bob arrived at the Shrimp Galore parking lot. Betty was already there, so they walked hand in hand into the restaurant. Again, they asked to sit facing the entrance. Bob's friend on the start-up team, Fred Conway, had said they had the best fried shrimp in Houston, so he ordered the fried shrimp basket. Fred apparently ate there frequently, and he told Bob the owner went by the name *Shrimpy*. Betty started to order a salad, but the aroma of the frying shrimp made her decide to follow Bob's lead.

While waiting for their orders, Bob asked if there had been any progress on the case.

Betty said, *"We're still running down a few leads, but basically we have not yet found the Tin Man. The FBI used facial recognition and identified him as Marcus Stalinbeck. They also discovered some interesting background on him. He has a technical background with a degree in chemical engineering from South Ural State University in Russia. His first five years after school, he was an instrument engineer in a refinery located south of Moscow. It is apparent that he has the skills necessary to disable shutdown systems and cause the fires and explosion at the olefins plant. We are dealing with a very clever and talented arsonist."*

Bob said, *"Wow! That's what I call progress. You now know exactly the arsonist you are looking for. Have you managed to tie him to John Swisher?"*

Betty said, *"We are still working on that."*

Bob then said, *"Let me tell you how Swisher attacked me in a meeting!"*

Bob then told Betty about the confrontation with John Swisher during the monthly status review meeting. Although she had not found any direct connections between Swisher and Stalinbeck, the confrontation put him back in first place as a suspect. They had discovered Swisher's multiple calls to a burner phone prior to the fires and explosion, but anyone can buy an unlisted phone nowadays and throw it away after use. She said that what she needed was some sort of direct connection between the two men.

The shrimp baskets arrived, and they dug in. Absolutely delicious! Bob said he would have to remember to thank Fred Conway for the recommendation. The manager stopped by to see if they were enjoying their meal, and Bob surprised him by asking if he was Shrimpy. He gave a big smile, said he was, asking how Bob had known. When Fred Conway's name was mentioned, Shrimpy said that Fred was one of his best customers, and asked Bob to say hi to him from Shrimpy. Bob and Betty continued consuming the wonderful shrimp.

Bob said, *"Now I know why Fred has the weight problem!"*

Betty laughed and said, *"And if we keep this up, we'll have the same problem!"*

Suddenly, Betty looked up—and her facial expression indicated there was something wrong. Coming in the entrance was a large woman with a drawn pistol, looking around the restaurant.

Betty quickly drew her weapon and shouted, *"Stop, put down your weapon, or I'll shoot!"* The woman raised her pistol into firing position, and Betty fired three shots, hitting her twice in the chest and once in the forehead. She went down like a sack of potatoes. The restaurant went nuts at that point, with people running in every direction. Betty quickly quieted the situation, identifying herself as a police officer. She then called for backup and a forensic team.

While waiting for backup to arrive, Betty searched the woman for identification—there was none. She was, however, carrying her cell phone—a bad mistake. She determined that the woman was wearing body armor that prevented the first two shots from killing her. However, the shot to the middle of the forehead took care of that. Fortunately, there were several individuals who witnessed the woman entering the restaurant with a drawn weapon, and who recalled Betty's warning.

Betty suggested to the restaurant owner that he give customers doggie boxes to take their food home. Bob thought that was amusing considering the panic that had occurred a few minutes earlier. Surprisingly, most folks did take the food home—another indication of the great shrimp! The owner told the customers that it was all on the house—and said, *"This doesn't happen every day. Please come back!"*

When the forensic team arrived, they taped off the restaurant and began to gather evidence. They interviewed five people who said they had seen the woman enter with a drawn gun and heard the policewoman's warning. Present-day technology allows fingerprints to be taken at the scene, so they quickly identified the woman as Penny Lusher, a known hit man (woman) that the FBI had been looking for. This seemed quite logical since she was wearing body armor. Both Bob and Betty indicated to the investigating team that she was aiming in their direction when Betty decided to shoot.

The forensic team finished and left the restaurant. Betty thanked the owner, Shrimpy, for his cooperation. Bob, trying to lighten the mood, said he was upset because he knocked over his shrimp basket. Shrimpy insisted on them taking two new shrimp baskets with them.

Bob said, *"If it is always this exciting eating here, I'm coming back!"*

He got a small smile out of Shrimpy for that, and he said, *"I hope you eat here as often as Fred Conway does!"*

Betty had asked one of the forensic team who lived close to her apartment to drive her car back to the police station, and pick her up the next morning. She rode with Bob back to her apartment. On the way, she said that she already had someone looking for anything in common between the Tin Man and the Hit Woman. For some reason, Betty's use of the aliases seemed humorous, and Bob had to pull over he was laughing so hard. It may have been his way of relieving the tension from the murder attempt on his life. After he recovered, and they were back on the road, Betty said she had them searching Penny Lusher's phone records to see how the phone had been used and where it had been used. Betty said they would try to find out where she had been staying and get a search warrant. Bob asked if Betty had any enemies that were out to kill her. She said, *"No killer enemies, but I've got to start being more selective about my lunch companions!"* There wasn't any question in her mind that Bob had been the target. This was try number 4. She said, *"Bob, you have used four of your nine lives—let's not use any more!"*

When they arrived at Betty's apartment building, Bob walked her up to her door. A parting kiss had become almost standard for them, but when Betty approached, Bob knelt down on the concrete. Betty said, *"What are you up to?"*

Bob said, *"I had planned to do this at a fancy restaurant, with romantic music playing. But today, I realized how much I love you. If you had been shot in that restaurant, my life would have been over. Betty, I can't live without you. Please accept this engagement ring and marry me."*

Betty was surprised, but said, *"I love you too. I will marry you—but you must promise me not to get assassinated before the wedding!"* Bob was okay with that restriction and placed the ring on Betty's finger; they embraced, and had a long passionate kiss.

Outside Betty's apartment, there were a few benches. They sat on one and hugged, kissed, and discussed their future. Although Bob had met Betty's parents, she planned to invite them all to dinner to break the news about the engagement. Bob's parents lived in upstate New York, so he would break the news over the telephone. Then they would have a FaceTime phone call to do the "in person" introductions. They both were on the same page, wanting two or three kids. Both of them wished the evening could go on forever, but being Christians wanting to obey their Lord, they parted company, waiting for the appropriate time to consummate their marriage.

The next morning, at head office Engineering, Bob was back in his normal routine. Except, of course, telling everyone he knew that he had asked Betty to marry him. There were congratulations all around. Ralph Swenson, Bob's boss, congratulated him and said that he had an engagement gift for him down in his office. That was a mystery, so he followed Ralph down the hall. Ralph sat behind his desk and again congratulated Bob on his engagement.

Then he said, *"My engagement gift is this: You are being returned to the Deer Park olefins plant for the start-up. Every day that you drive to work in five minutes rather than forty-five minutes, you can think, 'This is the gift Ralph gave me.' They have rebuilt the damaged areas, are running the final checks on the instrumentation, and will be starting up again within the week."* Bob thanked Ralph and promised to think of him every day when he was driving. He reminded him that at the end of the start-up he had been promised a permanent job at head office. Ralph said that he had done a great job, and that was still the plan.

The rest of the day, Bob was walking on air. Engaged! To the best, most beautiful girl in the world! And now he would be working only minutes away from her! Within seconds he was on the phone to tell Betty the good news. He asked her, *"You haven't changed your mind, have you?"* She said, "No," and informed him about everyone that she had told about the engagement.

Then she told him some news about the case. The fact that Penny Lusher, "the Hit Woman," had been carrying her cell phone had been a big mistake. By triangulating call records off cell towers, they were able to locate the hotel in which she had been staying. A search of the room confirmed her identification. She had made multiple calls to the same burner phone that John Swisher had called several times. The Massey VP and the Hit Woman were calling the same person—and it didn't take a genius to figure out who that was—the Tin Man. Again, by triangulation off several cell towers, it was learned about the rented room where the Tin Man had been staying. Unfortunately, he had moved on by the time they got there. They checked the trash dumpster and found Internet articles on arson, explosives, and, believe it or not, the same article Bob Garver had read on climbing chain-link fences. Lots of circumstantial evidence, but no solid proof that John Swisher had hired either individual for the fires or the hit. On the other hand, Swisher, the person of interest, became the prime suspect as the mastermind behind the Massey fires and explosion and the attempt on Bob's life.

CHAPTER 13

NOSE TO THE GRINDSTONE

Bob arrived at the olefins plant start-up trailer an hour early. His old desk was still there—with the same paperwork that was on it when he left. It was like stepping back in time. He hadn't been at the plant since the day he walked the perimeter chain-link fence and found the security problems. As expected, Jack Fishbane was sitting in his office going over a schedule. He looked up and said, *"You're early! We don't start until eight o'clock."*

Bob replied, *"Okay, I'll go home and come back at eight!"*

Jack laughed, then said, *"I'm glad to see you. We're about ready to start up again, and you are sorely needed."*

Bob replied, *"Let's see if we can start it up without burning it down this time!"*

Jack congratulated him on his engagement—apparently, the information was spreading.

Around 8:00 a.m., the other instrument engineers and instrument inspectors started coming in. Apparently, the shooting at Shrimp Galore had made the TV news. Bob's name had been included, but fortunately, there were no pictures other than a shot of the restaurant. Shrimpy's restaurant was getting some free advertising—maybe it would make up for yesterday's lost business. Bob was getting a reputation as the Clint Eastwood of the olefins plant. When this was mentioned, he said, *"Are ya feelin' lucky? Make my day!"* Everyone congratulated him on his engagement, and there were handshakes all around. Then everybody got busy. Jack Fishbane scheduled a 9:00 a.m. status meeting, mainly to bring Bob up to speed on the approaching start-up.

In the meeting, Fred Conway was the first to provide an update. His three high-pressure boilers were ready to start. The Controls Inc. instrument technicians had been sent to two weeks of training on the new firing sequence controls, and the nuisance shutdowns were expected to stop—without having an instrument engineer present when any work was done. Jack Fishbane said, *"That's what it says in the book—but the first shutdown, we'll be back on the instrument engineer wake-up schedule!"*

Since Jack had the next area to start up, the pyrolysis furnaces, process gas compressors, and gasoline hydrotreater, he gave the next update. The fire damage from the electrical fire outside the control room and the hydrogen flange fire had been repaired and started up prior to the other fires. The massive process gas compressor fire caused by the three-inch block valve being left open had been repaired and was having its final instrumentation checks done. The gasoline hydrotreater repairs had been completed, checked out, and it was ready for start-up. Bob joked that on his way in this morning, it was good to see the GHT heater standing upright for a change. He said, *"Let's keep it that way! It was kind of weird seeing it tilted at twenty degrees!"*

Because Bob had been on assignment at head office, Jack covered the refrigeration and separation areas of the plant, for which Bob was responsible. Most of those sections had not been started up prior to the fires and explosion. Jack indicated that the instrumentation had been checked out prior to the original start-up; however, they were repeating that checkout as a precaution, and it was within hours of completion. In other words, all areas were ready for start-up. He said Bob had a few minor change orders to get done prior to start-up, and he would pass them on after the meeting.

Following the meeting, Jack met with Bob in his office to transfer some small ongoing projects. The most urgent was a modification to the instrumentation design for the instrument air system. This vintage plant relied on instrument quality air to run the instruments. Electronic instruments were on the horizon, but as yet, they had not captured the majority of new projects. The issue was related to an override circuit. The main air header was under pressure control, set at 110 PSIG. But usually there was an override. An override circuit normally operates "out of the way," but when a limit is exceeded, it takes over control.

One of the overrides on the instrument air was a moisture controller. The air driers were supposed to maintain the dew point of the instrument air around minus forty degrees Fahrenheit. Pneumatic instruments demand clean dry air, since they have very small orifices within the instruments that can clog up, causing failure. Liquid water is a killer to pneumatics, so if the dew point of the air rises above the outside temperature, liquid water condenses, and the entire plant can have problems at the same time. The moisture override was set to close the valve supplying instrument air to the plant.

At the same time, a low-pressure controller would introduce nitrogen (which is bone-dry) to keep the pressure up for the instrumentation. If this ever occurred, an emergency alarm was to sound in the control room to warn operators to quickly put on Scott Air-Paks and send others out of the control building so they would not get asphyxiated. Unessential personnel were instructed to stay out of the control room until the instrument air had been reestablished and the oxygen level was again above 20 percent. Operators were assigned to stand at the entrance and keep anyone from entering.

Apparently, when the plant was designed, the moisture analyzer was installed, but the moisture override had not been implemented. The problem for Bob was that it must be done "online"—while the instrument air system was running. Jack warned Bob that if the cutover took too long, it could shut everything down that was already up and running and cause evacuation of the control building.

Bob looked at the problem and determined that since the pressure controller used an air to open valve, a low-pressure selector would have to be "cut into" the pneumatic tubing behind the panel so that high moisture would close the instrument air pressure valve. Most of the override could be built ahead of time. The low-pressure selector could be mounted, but the actual cutover would have to be done quickly to avoid the control valve going closed for too long.

The nitrogen pressure controller had been installed during construction and was ready to supply nitrogen if the instrument air failed; however, since it was an emergency condition to supply nitrogen to the control room, it would be blocked in prior to the cutover. Obviously, with nitrogen unavailable, if the cutover was messed up, the entire running plant would shut down due to low instrument air pressure.

It took Bob a few days to design the system and get the new low-pressure override mounted in a convenient location for the cutover. He held a meeting with the utilities process engineer, Lyle Talbot, and his operations foreman to go over the cutover strategy. He thought everyone was on board. The day came for the cutover. The nitrogen was blocked in by the operator. The moment of truth had arrived.

Bob had briefed the two instrument technicians on exactly how the cutover would be made. Fortunately, the panel was tubed using hand-tightened Imperial Eastman fittings. The tube from the pressure controller output to the field bulkhead would have to be replaced by the low-pressure selector. New tubing had been run from the low-pressure selector to the controller output and to the field bulkhead. Two technicians would be used—one to disconnect the field bulkhead and connect the new tubing, and one to disconnect the controller output and reconnect the new tubing. Bob reviewed the procedure several times with the two men.

The time had come. Lyle Talbot, the process engineer, was at the front of the panel. Bob discussed the issue with him, and he stated that if the cutover was not done within thirty seconds, it would probably shut the plant down. Bob moved to oversee the work behind the panel, and believe it or not, Lyle shouted, *"Ready, set, go!"* Lyle started counting down from thirty (Bob felt like going out and strangling him!). The bulkhead cutover went smoothly without problem; however, the technician making the controller output connection dropped the pneumatic tubing female connector, and it rolled under the flooring. Panic!

Fortunately, Bob had thought of everything—he reached in his pocket and pulled out a few of that type of connector. The technician was shaking too badly to be of much help, so Bob made the connection himself. The pipefitters union might not approve, but it had to be done. He quickly ran to the front of the panel in time to hear Lyle count, "Five, four, three, two, one." Checking the pressure controller, the instrument valve was open, and under control. Whew! They ran a quick check of the moisture controller overriding the pressure valve, and it worked perfectly. Bob told Lyle, *"Who says instrument engineering is boring! And by the way, you aren't invited to the next hot cutover!"*

Bob turned around, and who should he see "lurking" on the other side of the control room? Jack Fishbane. Jack came over and congratulated him on the cutover.

Bob cynically commented, *"I couldn't have done it without Lyle counting down!"*

The instrument technician who had dropped the fitting said, *"Yeah, we couldn't have survived without that!"*

Bob made sure the operator knew he had to open the nitrogen valve back up and then close the work order.

Another day, another dollar!

CHAPTER 14

STUFF HAPPENS

Bob's assumed his normal routine, preparing for his area to start up. Fred Conway's high-pressure boilers were starting up, this time without the shutdowns they had experienced before the instrument technicians had been trained on the new system. Being sadistic, Bob longed for the days when Bud Asperson, the utilities manager, would come running into the trailer yelling at Fred. No—not really!

Jack Fishbane's pyrolysis furnaces were coming up at a rate of one per day, and the rebuilt process gas compressor area was handling the gas without problems. It looked like this was the rainbow at the end of the storm. Jack's gasoline hydrotreater was to start the next day. The rewelded lines had been pressure tested, and everything looked good. Then, to everyone's chagrin, a loud boom sounded. Around ten minutes later, Fred Conway and John Cross, the start-up electrical engineer, came running into the start-up trailer. Both looked like they had seen a ghost.

Fred explained that they had been walking on their way to check out some wiring on the demineralizer. As they walked under a utilities pipe rack, the loud boom occurred, and a three-inch valve, with a portion of its attached pipe, buried itself in the ground about ten feet from them. John Cross commented, *"I would never have guessed that Fred and I could scale a five-foot concrete wall! But that's what we did. We both jumped over the concrete tank farm barrier as we ran away from the area.*" Fred's FRCs (fire retardant clothing) were wet, confirming that the explosion had also caused some laundry problems.

The Safety Department was immediately on top of the problem, and this time it was not the Tin Man's fault. Liquid nitrogen is supplied to the plant by the truckload and stored in a large heavily insulated vessel. The liquid nitrogen is then heated to turn it into a gas prior to sending it to the plant for various uses. Liquid nitrogen has a boiling point of –320°F. Since the coldest temperature possible is 459.67°F, that's "mighty cold." Liquid that cold requires a material that can stand up to the temperature—and 316 stainless steel was selected in the design. However, once the nitrogen is warmed enough to turn into a gas, the temperature allows the use of carbon steel, which is much less expensive. *But* if somehow the liquid nitrogen comes in contact with the carbon steel, it becomes weak and brittle.

It was determined that was what had happened. But how? Because the temperature controller on the nitrogen heat exchanger had closed the low-pressure steam to the exchanger. But why? Because an operator climbing around on the piping had stepped on the tubing going to the air to open valve, breaking it off. Tubing is not meant to be a ladder! Within a few minutes, with no heat on the nitrogen heater, the liquid nitrogen worked its way through the exchanger, embrittled the carbon steel pipe, and boom—Fred Conway's FRCs were wet! Fortunately, tubing is easy to repair, three-inch carbon steel pipe is readily available, and they had everything up and working within a couple of hours. No other parts of the plant needed to shut down. Everyone breathed a sigh of relief.

It wasn't long before the refrigeration compressors were needed for the hydrocarbon separation section of the olefins plant. This was Bob Garver's area. These compressors used the same high-pressure steam to drive their compressor turbines that the process gas compressors did. Although huge, these machines were comparable to a home air conditioner compressor—the principle remains the same. The refrigerant is pressured up by the compressor. It is then let down (reduced in pressure) through a valve. The expansion of the gas causes it to get very cold, and the cold refrigerant is circulated through heat exchangers to cool various products. As it warms up, it is circulated back to the suction of the compressor, where the cycle repeats itself.

The remainder of the hydrocarbon separation section consists of distillation columns, which separate the heavy products from the lighter products. The basic principle is that as you cool a gas, liquid starts to drop out, and the liquid contains the heavier components. Distillation columns consist of many "trays" that are used to separate the gas from the liquid phase. The liquid flows down the column, cooling the upcoming gas. The gas flows upward, finally exiting the column at the top. There is a final separation of liquid from the gas in an overhead vessel, and the liquid captured there is recycled back to the distillation column for cooling. The energy that drives the process is derived in a heat exchanger at the bottom of the column, called a reboiler, which heats the liquid that reaches the bottom of the column. The feed to be separated generally comes into the column on one of the trays about three-fourths of the way up the column. These complex separation columns are what chemical engineers dream about! Or maybe have nightmares about!

The distillation columns are generally named for the product produced. In an olefins plant, there is an ethane column, a propane column, a propylene column, an ethylene column, and several others. These components are only liquid at very low temperatures. This is the function of the refrigeration compressors—to cool the gas way down, and then use slightly higher temperatures (still mighty cold) to "heat" the distillation columns and produce the separation. The refrigerated streams flow through heavily insulated pipes, passing through a large metal box called a "cold box." Packed inside the cold box are multiple heat exchangers that are totally enclosed in pellets of insulating material (usually perlite). Very little heat gets in from the outside, so the cold box can hold very low temperatures.

Bob Garver was told that a valve regulating one of the cold box flows was controlled by a temperature controller that read a thermocouple transmitter whose thermocouple was buried deep in the cold box. This application was a big user of the refrigerant coming from the refrigeration compressors. The design used a separate pneumatic shutdown transmitter whose output triggered a pneumatic shutdown relay. This relay, when tripped, would close a refrigerant shutdown valve by venting the air to the valve operator. The trip set point had never been tested, and a work order had been written to make sure it was set correctly. This was a risky job since the refrigerant was running, and the valve itself must not be closed. The risk of a shutdown was recognized, but no one realized how much of a shutdown that would be.

Recognizing the risk involved, Bob wrote a detailed procedure for setting the trip point. Bob required that the instrument technician "split ring" the valve stem to keep it from going closed (fail closed valve). This required the technician to measure the distance from the valve packing to the valve stem connector, cut a piece of conduit that length, split it horizontally, and wire it onto the valve stem. This would make it impossible for the valve to close in case the testing went sour. Well, long story short, the instrument technician thought he knew better, believing he could achieve the same thing by limiting the air to the valve positioner. In fact, this was the wrong direction, and he managed to close the shutdown valve. By the time he recognized his mistake, all heck had broken loose.

By the time Bob was called to investigate, most of the plant was shut down. It was like a row of dominoes set up by a kid. The first domino falls, and before long, all the dominoes are down. The refrigerant valve shutdown caused the refrigeration compressor controls to start swinging. This cycled the high-pressure steam that supplied both the refrigeration compressor and the process gas compressor. That caused the process gas compressor controls to start cycling, which caused major additional changes in the high-pressure steam header. The boilers could not keep up with the huge changes in demand for high-pressure steam, and they shut down—one on high steam pressure, and another on low level. Without high-pressure steam, everything began to shut down. The plant shutdown cost Massey over $100,000.

Understandably, operations was upset, and once they discovered that the instrument technician had caused the whole thing, a hurricane of anger was headed for the instrument start-up trailer. It was Bob Garver's turn to face the wrath of Operations, in the form of Rich Michaels, the separation section operations manager—worse than the Wrath of Khan. Bob discovered that the instrument technician at fault was "Long John" Whippet, one of the crew he first worked with on the demineralizer valve the first night after he reported for work at Deer Park. He brought Long John in to see how it had happened. The guy was apologetic, but recognized he was in big trouble. He admitted he had not followed the instructions to split ring the valve, since he thought he had a better way. Bob told him that he should have consulted with him before deviating from the instructions, and explained why the "better way" had caused the valve to close, starting the dominoes to fall.

Jack Fishbane was brought up to speed on the cause of the plant shutdown, and at Operations' request, he was ready to get Whippet fired. Bob reminded him that Long John was one of the best instrument technicians that Controls, Inc. had, and this was the first time he had caused any problems—although admittedly, this one was a dilly! It seemed obvious that he would never make the mistake of not following instructions again.

Bob's father had worked for a large pharmaceutical company. And he used to tell the story about a guy who opened the wrong valve and sent $250,000 worth of drugs into the sewer. The guy was about to be fired when the president of the company came up and said, *"No way— he's just had $250,000 worth of training! We can't waste that!"*

Bob said to Jack Fishbane, *"Whippet has just had $100,000 worth of training. Let's not waste that!"*

Everyone saw the point, and Long John Whippet's job was saved. Word got around, and all of the Controls, Inc. technicians thought Bob could do no wrong.

One "tiny" advantage—since the plant was down for a few hours, it was easy to check the temperature trip that had caused the whole thing—no problem opening and closing the valve now. Bob made sure that Long John did the work, and he gave it his personal attention.

CHAPTER 15

INTRODUCTIONS AND CONFRONTATION

Bob had agreed to have dinner with Betty's parents at Purdy's Steak House. She indicated that she would pick them up at their hotel, and they would meet him at the restaurant at 7:00 p.m. When he arrived, he found that they had already been seated. Since Betty had arranged for a table having a view of the door, he had no problem finding them. Betty introduced him to her parents, John and Marsha Marcum. Bob and John shook hands, and Bob sat down between Betty and Marsha. To make conversation, Bob asked John what he did for a living. John said that he was retired but had owned a small computer sales and installation store in Cleveland, Texas, where they lived. Bob said that he had started using computers during the Apple IIe era—that his first IBM computer only had 10 meg of memory, with eight-inch floppy disks; and he now was using the latest and greatest Dell offering. This provided an opportunity for conversation around a common interest.

Marsha Marcum had been a stay-at-home mom and had raised Betty and her brother, Bill, who was attending Texas A&M University, studying for a degree in civil engineering. Both parents were obviously very proud of their two kids. John said, *"Betty has told us you work at Massey Chemical Company, but she wasn't sure exactly what you do."* Bob told them that he was a graduate chemical engineer but had never practiced chemical engineering. He explained that immediately after leaving school, he went to work for an instrumentation manufacturer and had become what is referred to as an instrument engineer or process control engineer.

Since most folks have no idea what an instrument engineer does, Bob used the example of a home thermostat to explain what a controller's function is, as one example of an instrument. He said, *"It reads your home's temperature, has a set point (where you want the temperature to be), and basically turns the heater or air conditioner on and off to keep the home at the set point temperature."* He explained that a chemical plant is chock-full of controllers similar to that—controlling level, pressure, speed, etc. as well as temperature.

Betty suggested that her parents might be getting bored with Bob's long-winded explanation. They denied it, but the conversation moved on to Betty's work at the Deer Park Police Department. Although she had been in the department for seven years, and her parents had a good grasp of what she did, they had questions about her new assignment as a police lieutenant. She explained. *"The difference involves working on higher-level cases. Before, in addition to routine patrols, I would be called out on 'plain-vanilla' cases like domestic disputes, noisy parties, vandalism, even cats up in trees. But as a lieutenant, I take on cases like breaking and entering, robbery, assault, or even murder."*

Marsha Marcum expressed concern for her daughter's safety, but Betty said that 99 percent of her time was just boring paperwork. She said, *"Police work consists of hours and hours of boredom, separated by a few minutes of sheer terror."* That didn't do much to soothe her mother.

The menus arrived, and Betty used this time to explain that this restaurant was where she and Bob had gone on their first date. She said that she remembered having the petit filet, which was excellent. Bob recommended that John try the Purdy pork chops, leaving off the fact that it was a huge dinner, resembling a pork roast more than pork chops. When the waiter returned, since all dinners came with a house tossed salad, and steamed vegetables, there was no need for further decisions.

While they waited for their meals, Marsha asked Betty and Bob if they had decided on a wedding date. Betty said, *"We're thinking about a December wedding since the Houston area will be cooler then, and it could add a special Christmas theme for the wedding. We are also thinking about a honeymoon in New Zealand, since that would be their summertime."* This set the two women off excitedly talking and planning. Bob and John rolled their eyes at each other, but sat there like bumps on a log.

Bob commented, *"Men aren't really needed at all in a wedding! And their opinions aren't of much value."* John agreed.

Their meals arrived, and John remarked, *"You set me up! This isn't a pork chop! It's a pork roast cut into ten pork chops!"*

Bob laughed and said, *"If you can't finish it, you can take it back to the hotel for breakfast—or Betty can take it home to her Shih Tzu, Robber."*

Marsha remarked that if John ate the whole thing, he would explode, and that it would take both Betty's dog, Robber, and her cat, Bandit, to eat all that meat. Everybody dug in, and the meal was thoroughly enjoyed by all. When the waiter came to see if they wanted dessert, John and Marsha said they were full; but Betty romantically suggested that each couple share a bananas foster like they had on their first date. Her parents couldn't resist that appeal—and they all managed to "force it down" some way, enjoying it immensely.

When the waiter came with the check, the two men both wanted to pay. But Bob recognized that it was a father's prerogative to be top dog during this first meeting, so he graciously accepted, insisting that he handle the tip. While waiting for the waiter to come back, conversation turned to Betty's present case involving the arson and explosion at Massey Chemical. She gave her parents the bare-bones description of the case, indicating that it involved several fires and one explosion at the chemical plant that were caused by an arsonist. They had identified the arsonist but had not yet been able to find him. She then tread lightly explaining that Bob was a witness who had seen the arsonist at the scene of the first fire and that he had been attacked because of it. She didn't mention that there had actually been four attacks. She ended her description of the case by saying to Bob, *"Give me a call tomorrow. We have some more information we need to go over."*

As they all walked to the parking lot, Betty did a scan of the area, but didn't see anything suspicious. Conversation turned to how the Houston Rockets were doing. It looked like they might just make the playoffs. John suggested that maybe they could all attend a game in the near future. They got in their cars and went their separate ways. All in all, it had been a successful and pleasant first meeting. That did not always happen when a new fiancé met the girl's parents. Which reminded Bob—he and Betty still had to have the phone call with his parents to announce their engagement, but that would wait for another day.

The next day, at 8:00 a.m., Bob called Betty at the police station to find out what news she had on the case. She said, *"Bob, I've whacked the hornet's nest. I went to see Vice President John Swisher again."*

Bob said, *"Oh, oh—I need to start carrying my weapon. What did you say to him?"*

Betty said, *"I told him that there had been an attempted assassination of the arson case witness in a restaurant in South Houston. He said, 'What does that have to do with me?' I told him we had the assassin's cell phone, and asked him, 'Why did you call that number?' His face turned white, and he denied calling it, saying that he didn't even know whose number it was. I told him we have his phone records, and he did indeed call that number. He said that someone must have used his phone while he wasn't around. I said, 'Three times over three days?'*

"I asked outright, 'Did you hire that person to kill the witness?' Again, he turned white and said the phone company must have messed up. I said, 'Yeah, right.' I then dropped the final hammer. I said, 'What if I told you that the Massey Chemical plant arsonist called that same number several times prior to the fires and explosion? And what if I told you that you made several calls to the phone that he called from? How would you explain that?' At that point, he stood up and told me to leave—he said he was calling his lawyer and would not answer any more questions. Bob, does that sound like an innocent man?"

Bob was amazed that Betty had made so much progress on the case. He asked her if she planned on arresting Swisher.

She said, *"Unfortunately, no. It isn't illegal to make a call to a burner phone. But we're not through with Swisher—we have a warrant to look deeper into his finances. Somehow, money had to be transferred to purchase the hit at Shrimp Galore. If we ever find the Tin Man, I can guarantee he will turn State's evidence against Swisher to save his skin."*

Betty suggested that since the hornet's nest was buzzing, Bob needed to take every precaution. He said that he normally placed a 9 mm pistol in his glove compartment but had purchased another gun and a magnetic holder placed under the dash to make it easily accessible. He also planned to conceal carry whenever possible—it would not be possible while at the olefins plant. Betty told him to call her immediately if he ran into any problems.

They ended their phone conversation by agreeing to meet for the phone call with Bob's parents on Saturday. Bob suggested that they follow that with a day at the Houston Zoo—Betty agreed that would be cool.

CHAPTER 16

FACETIME AND TRIP TO THE ZOO

Bob spent the rest of the workweek solving problems that came up during the start-up of his area in the olefins plant. Overall, the start-up was finally going quite well, and there had been no additional events that were suspicious. The instrument engineers were on shift duty for the weekend, but Bob had arranged to be off on Saturday. He was looking forward to the trip to the Houston Zoo.

Bob and Betty had agreed that making the FaceTime call to his parents from Bob's apartment would be the best location, since Betty's roommate, Cindy Parker, was home on Saturdays. Bob's father was retired from a large pharmaceutical company. His mother was involved in church work. Therefore, Bob sometimes had difficulty reaching them by phone. He had texted both of them and sent an email asking them to be available at 10:00 a.m. on Saturday to talk with him and Betty. They both said they would be at home for the call.

Bob picked up Betty at her apartment at 9:00 a.m. and headed for his apartment. Betty was anxious about meeting his parents, even though it was by FaceTime. If the truth be known, Bob was a bit anxious himself. He was unsure about how they would react. At 10:00 a.m., Bob started the FaceTime program and turned on the computer speaker. He dialed his parents' number, and they picked up almost immediately. Bob started the conversation with the typical *"How are you? What's the weather like?"* etc. etc. It was apparent that he was delaying the inevitable.

Finally, his father said, *"So what's this call about? It was a rather formal request you made via email. What's going on?"*

Bob replied, *"Dad, Mom. I'm getting married. I would like to introduce my fiancée, Betty Marcum."*

Betty moved into camera range and said, *"Hello, Mr. and Mrs. Garver. I'm sure this is a shock to you, but Bob and I have been dating for about five months, and we decided last week to get married. I want to meet you in person soon, and I hope we have your blessing."*

Bob's mother said, *"We were guessing about the phone call and suspected this might be the reason. We have all the confidence in the world in Bob's judgment. If he has asked you to marry him, we know you must be a fine person."*

Bob's father added, *"Congratulations, you two! When is the wedding?"*

Bob said, *"Although we are still working out the details, it looks like it will be a December wedding, here in Deer Park. I have started attending the church that Betty belongs to—Faith Community Church. Pastor Lancy will do the honors at the wedding. He teaches verse by verse from the Bible, and that is what Betty and I prefer."*

Betty said, *"We'll let you know the details as soon as they are firm. I hope you will be able to attend."*

Bob's father replied, *"Wild horses couldn't keep us away! Let me know if there is anything we can do to help out."*

The conversation then turned to describing Betty's job as a police lieutenant, her education, where she was raised, her parents, and other details in which her future parents-in-law were interested. Bob was finally relaxing—the FaceTime call had gone smoothly, and he was no longer anxious. Surprisingly, Betty was starting to feel comfortable talking with these "strangers." Bob's parents said that, as soon as the wedding date was fixed, they would start planning their trip from upstate New York.

Bob suggested that they might want to make a vacation out of it, travelling down the east coast and west along the gulf coast. He said they might want to stop in Washington, DC, since that was where they had spent their honeymoon. He also knew his mother loved flowers, so he added that Bellingrath Gardens, outside Mobile, Alabama, would be an interesting stop. They seemed interested in the idea, and it was obvious that they both were starting to plan the trip in their minds. The call came to an end, and Betty said she would call when the wedding date was firm.

Bob sat back on the sofa—he had been sitting on the edge, being concerned about the call. Betty had also been tense, but now she settled back next to Bob and said, *"Wow! Your parents are great! That call went much better than I feared."*

Bob replied, *"Betty, I can tell you now, I was a bit concerned about it myself. But they loved you! Paul was right in Philippians: 'Be anxious for nothing, but in everything by prayer and supplication with thanksgiving let your requests be made known to God.' I can tell you now, I've been praying about the call."*

Betty snuggled up close and said, *"Me too! Let's head for the zoo!"*

Bob said, *"I didn't know you were a poet!"*

On the drive to the Houston Zoo, it seemed like they discussed a million items about their upcoming wedding. Where would they live? Since Betty had a roommate, it seemed logical that Betty move into Bob's apartment. But Betty suggested that maybe moving to "new digs" would make a clean break from the past. They agreed that a small family of two or three children fit their view of the future—of course, they wanted at least one boy and one girl. They planned to continue attending Faith Community Church and get involved in their Young Couples group. Both of them thought having received Christ as Savior established a rock-solid basis for their marriage. Having solved all the problems in the world, they finally arrived at the Houston Zoo parking lot.

The Houston Zoo is a fifty-five-acre zoological park located within Hermann Park in Houston, Texas. The zoo houses over six thousand animals from nine hundred species. It receives 2.1 million visitors each year and is the second most visited zoo in the United States. Since Bob and Betty were visiting on a Saturday, the zoo had an average-sized crowd. Betty noted that during the week, groups of schoolchildren were present, sometimes making it difficult to see all the animals.

Bob paid for their tickets at the entrance, which was easy to find, having a huge Zoo ENTRANCE sign in multiple colors over the gate. They hadn't eaten breakfast, so they stopped at the Cyprus Circle Café for sweet rolls and coffee.

* * *

It was getting warm, so as they passed the sea lions pool, Bob said, *"I think I'll cool you off by throwing you in with the sea lions!"*

Betty patted her concealed pistol and replied, *"If you think you're big enough, buster!"* They had a good laugh over that.

Bob wanted to tour the Reptile House, but Betty nixed that, saying, *"Eve got into all kinds of trouble dealing with a snake—I'm not about to repeat her mistake!"* Bob laughed, and they went on to the Tropical Birdhouse.

He said, *"Birds are okay? There were birds in the Garden of Eden."* It was Betty's turn to laugh. On the way, they saw an Asian elephant and a lemur.

Betty said, *"That elephant is how big I'm going to be if I keep going to all those restaurants you have me eating in."*

Bob told her that she would still be the most beautiful woman on earth, even if she was as big as an elephant. She said, *"You smooth talker you."*

After the Tropical Birdhouse, which had thousands of birds, they saw the alligators, a bald eagle, and took a ride on the Wildlife Carousel. In the back part of the zoo, they saw and fed the giraffes, marveled at the rhino, and spent fifteen minutes watching the chimpanzees. One of the chimpanzees seemed intrigued by Betty and put on a show, sticking out his tongue at her. She returned the compliment, and he did cartwheels for her. They left the chimpanzees still laughing at their antics.

On the return trip, they saw a gorilla (Betty compared him to Bob), a huge Galapagos turtle, and a black bear. Betty commented that most animals were in areas similar to their natural habitat. Bob said, *"Maybe they should build an apartment building and put humans in here."* Next they passed by the lions, the tigers, and the cougars. At the cougars exhibit, there were several young people in University of Houston Cougars tee shirts making clever comments about their mascot.

On the way back to the entrance, they again passed by the Reptile House. By this time, Betty had built up her courage, and they decided to go in. It seemed like they had every kind of poisonous snake on the planet, as well as ugly iguanas, etc.

When they came out, Betty said, *"I can sum that up in one word. YUK!"*

Bob laughed and promised they would avoid reptiles from now on. The trip around the zoo had taken two hours, and they didn't even see everything. Bob had been to the Philadelphia and San Diego zoos, but Houston's zoo was very impressive.

After the zoo, they decided to be silly and ride the Hermann Park Railroad. It was primarily intended for children, but they enjoyed the ride, and it gave them an overview of the park area. After that, they rented a paddleboat and paddled around the small McGovern Lake—kind of interesting paddling around a lake surrounded by tall buildings. They then decided to walk around McGovern Gardens, which was built to celebrate Hermann Park's one hundredth year. The rose garden was outstanding.

*   *   *

Since it was getting toward dinnertime, they stopped at the Pinewood Café and had their "build-your-own grilled cheese sandwiches" accompanied by strawberry smoothies.

Betty said, *"Like I told you, Bob, we're both going to be the size of that elephant if we keep eating this way."*

Bob said, *"Just more of you to love! And ain't it great—these sandwiches are super!"*

On the way out of the park, they passed by Miller Outdoor Theater. Bob said that they should plan to attend one of their presentations. They decided to get out and walk around the theater, so they parked in the unoccupied lot. They found that the theater has seats available under a canopy, but many folks just bring a blanket and sit out on the lawn; and best of all, the lawn is free. But waiting for cooler weather seemed like the best plan for Houston's heat and humidity. It had been a wonderful day for Bob and Betty, and they would never forget it.

When they arrived back at the parking lot, Betty noticed a second car was parked on the other side of the lot. A man got out of the car and pointed something at them. Betty threw herself against Bob, knocking him to the ground as several shots rang out. Betty drew her weapon, and as they fell, she returned fire, but it was ineffectual. By this time, Bob had recovered and drawn his weapon. He fired three rounds at the assailant as he got into his car, peeled rubber, and zoomed out of the parking lot, heading up Main Street toward the Southwest Freeway. Bob was sure that at least two rounds hit the car. Unfortunately, the car was so far away, no license plate could be read. The best they could do was that it was a dark-colored sedan. That wouldn't be of much help. But there was no doubt in either of their minds: *"The Tin Man is still in town."* And apparently, he had been following them.

On the drive back to Betty's apartment, she noted that this was the fifth attack.

She said, *"I'm going to have to work 'firing while falling' into my range practice."*

Bob said, *"It looks like both of us could use more range time, but I think I hit his car with a couple of rounds. That may help locate it."*

In this attack, and the one on Smith Street, the Tin Man had used the Southwest Freeway for his escape. It was possible that might indicate the area of the city in which he was hiding. She said she would have a couple of her people take a picture of Marcus Stalinbeck (alias Tin Man) to the hotels along that freeway to see if anyone recognized him. That was a big job, and would take several days, but it was the best they had at this point.

They separated with a passionate kiss at Betty's apartment, and Bob said he would call her to say he had gotten home okay. He told her that he planned to sleep late, since he had the 4:00–12:00 shift at the olefins plant the next day. With the Tin Man on the loose, every moment seemed precious.

CHAPTER 17

FOLLOW THE MONEY AND COUNSELING

Betty spent the next day focusing on where John Swisher kept his money, and looking for suspicious money transfers. As you hear on TV crime shows so often, "Follow the money." Her department was blessed with a young police officer, Mack Turner, who could hack into just about any computer system. It was a good thing he was with the police—he would have made a criminal who was difficult to catch. Other officers referred to him jokingly as Mack the Hack. Previously, due to the amount of suspicious evidence she had obtained, Betty had obtained a warrant that was quite broad in scope allowing investigation of Swisher's finances. Betty asked Mack if he had found anything so far. He said that he had learned that Swisher had taken quite a lot of money out of the Massey company retirement savings fund and had been investing in rather risky stocks and even stock options.

Most folks have invested in stocks, either with the company they work for or by selecting stock on their own. However, very few people are knowledgeable enough to dabble in stock options. Mack tried to explain the difference in a simple way. He said that buying and selling stocks can be compared to betting on horses at the racetrack. At the end of the race, those who have bet on the correct horse to win, place, or show will make money. Those who bet on other horses will lose money. It's unlikely, but if everyone bets on the winning horse, they all win.

Trading options is more like gambling in a poker game. Each person bets against the other people in the game. But in the options game, the homeowner, where the game is held (the broker), takes a small cut for providing the facilities. The option buyer's gain is the option seller's loss and vice versa. It's important to remember that there are always two sides for every option transaction: a buyer and a seller. In other words, for every option purchased, there's always someone else selling it. If somebody wins, then somebody else lost.

Another important difference between stocks and options is that stocks give you a small piece of ownership in a company, while options are just contracts that give you the right to buy or sell at a specific price by a specific date. It is readily acknowledged that options trading is the more risky of the two.

John Swisher had been trading heavily in options, and was not very good at it—he had lost thousands of dollars. Betty noted that this would provide incentive for a gambler-type personality to "make it big" by selling stock short (another risky method), as he had done. And he could "guarantee" winning with insider information, in this case, taking action so that the stock dropped in value.

Mack also discovered that Swisher had an offshore bank account in the Cayman Islands. An offshore bank is a bank regulated under an international banking license. Due to less regulation and transparency, accounts with offshore banks are often used to hide undeclared income. Swisher had moved large amounts of money into this account on dates following the fires and explosion at Massey Chemical Co. Following the money backward, Mack found that the money was transferred from Swisher's brokerage account, following several short sales of Massey stock.

Betty asked Mack if there were any suspicious money transfers within the US. He pointed to several where Swisher had withdrawn a total of $50,000 in cash. But he had done so in $5,000 increments over ten days. Since the US Government gets interested in money transfers over $10,000, this looked very suspicious. The dates of these withdrawals started two weeks prior to the hit woman's attack at Shrimp Galore. Best information indicated that a hit can be bought for less than this amount.

The evidence was building.

Betty had invited Bob over to her apartment for dinner with her and her roommate, Cindy Parker. Cindy worked as a chef at Luby's, a family-friendly, cafeteria-style chain in the Houston area. Betty had told Bob that Cindy liked her job, but didn't like preparing the same food dishes every day. She was looking forward to trying a new recipe. Bob said he didn't mind being a guinea pig.

When he arrived at 7:00 p.m., he was greeted at the door of the apartment by both Betty and Cindy, who welcomed him graciously. They sat in the living room area and discussed their day's activities. Cindy brought out a bottle of Alsace Riesling in an ice bucket and poured a glass for each of them. It was fruity and dry—delicious. Bob asked Cindy what "gourmet feast" she had prepared for them. She indicated that she was trying a new recipe for quiche.

Bob joked, *"You know, real men don't eat quiche!"*

Betty said, *"I've tasted it—this will make a man out of you!"*

They all laughed. Betty mentioned that she had contacted the *Houston Chronicle* and given them an engagement announcement, which had appeared in that morning's paper. She asked if Bob had seen the announcement. Bob said he normally did not read "that biased rag," but in this case, he would make an exception and stop at the 7-Eleven to buy a paper.

When the conversation seemed to be winding down, Betty asked Cindy if it was all right with her if she brought Bob up to date on the arson case. Cindy said that was fine, she had to check dinner in the kitchen. Betty told Bob about John Swisher's losing options investments and his offshore bank accounts that received large inflows of money following his short sales of Massey stock. She included the information regarding the withdrawals of $50,000 in small amounts prior to the Shrimp Galore restaurant hit. Bob was amazed at how much progress had been made on the case. Betty gave Mack Turner most of the credit, joking that was why he was called Mack the Hack.

Bob asked if she planned to arrest Swisher soon. She said that nothing they had found so far was illegal. If they arrested everyone who made bad investments, the jails would be full. Having an offshore bank account was not illegal—it might interest the IRS, but there was nothing the local police were interested in.

Bob asked, *"How about the multiple withdrawals of $5,000?"*

Betty said that, again, there was nothing illegal about withdrawing your own money. The IRS might investigate this, but not the Deer Park Police. Bob was a bit frustrated, but Betty assured him that the evidence trail was building nicely. What they needed was to find Marcus Stalinbeck, "the Tin Man," and find the trail of money from Swisher to Stalinbeck.

"Dinner's ready!" Cindy called from the dining room. So Bob offered Betty his arm, and they strolled over to the table. After they were seated, Cindy asked Bob if he would say the blessing. He gladly obliged, asking God's blessing on the food, on Cindy the preparer, and on Betty and himself as they entered into marriage. Bob and Betty had been attending Faith Community Church for most of the time they had known each other. Betty had introduced Bob to this fellowship of Christians. Cindy had started attending about a month ago. When Bob asked her about it, she said that Betty had not only introduced her to the church, she had introduced her to Jesus Christ. Bob congratulated her on her decision and told her it was the most important decision of her lifetime.

The quiche was delicious, and slightly spicy. Bob complimented Cindy on it, and it was obvious she was pleased. She had prepared steamed vegetables as a side dish. Bob asked her about her job at Luby's. She said that it had been a great learning experience, especially regarding getting food out on a schedule. She said that she preferred to "dawdle" over her recipes, tasting them, adding various spices, and tasting again. At Luby's, the recipes were fixed, no modifications were allowed. She said that she was thinking about investigating other chef positions. Bob said, *"If this quiche is an example, you are destined to be a great chef!"*

Betty and Bob had begun attending the Young Couples Bible Study at church. They were studying the book of Daniel and its prophecies about the future. Cindy was in the Young Singles group who were doing a topical study about sexuality and marriage. She asked if Bob and Betty had scheduled marriage counseling yet. They indicated that they had not, but were planning on contacting Pastor Lancy about it. Cindy had been introduced to the idea in her Young Singles group and was sold on the idea. She said that it helps couples improve their relationships before marriage and after. They discuss such things as finances, communication, roles in marriage, affection and sex, children, family relationships, decision-making, dealing with anger, and many other topics.

Betty looked at Bob and said, *"That sounds great. What do you think?"*

Bob replied, *"Let's talk with Pastor Lancy about it. It should help us get to know each other better."*

Cindy added that many people go into marriage believing it will fulfill their social, financial, sexual, and emotional needs—and that's not always the case. By discussing differences and expectations before marriage, you can each better understand and support each other during marriage. She added that Pastor Lancy was licensed in Texas by the American Association for Marriage and Family Therapy.

Bob said, *"Betty, let's make sure we talk to Pastor Lancy about it next Sunday. And, Cindy, it sounds like you could run the sessions yourself!"* They all laughed.

For dessert, Cindy had made chocolate-covered strawberry cheesecakes in individual servings. The small cheesecakes were covered with milk chocolate and topped with a dab of whipped cream that supported a beautiful red strawberry. These were met with applause by Betty and Bob. Absolutely delicious!

After dinner, Bob volunteered to help with the dishes.

Cindy said, *"Betty, maybe you don't need the counseling—looks like Bob is trained right already. But no, Bob, we'll get the dishes later—let's sit down and have coffee."*

The coffee and conversation were great, and the pecan cookies that Cindy had baked were just right to finish the evening. Their discussions on a multitude of subjects solved most of the world's problems that night.

It was approaching 9:00 p.m., past Bob's normal bedtime, so he started dropping hints like, *"Well, I've got to get up early tomorrow."* so that they would start winding down the evening. The two gals picked up on the not-so-subtle hints and started clearing the cookies and coffee cups. Bob grabbed a couple of the pecan cookies for later—that pleased Cindy.

As Bob was leaving, he told Betty that he would call Pastor Lancy to confirm that they wanted marriage counseling. He asked her when she would be available, and they agreed that Sundays were almost always free. Since Cindy was still present, Bob gave Betty a perfunctory peck on the cheek as he was leaving.

Cindy said, *"Don't mind me! If you want to give her a romantic, passionate kiss, maybe I can learn something."*

They laughed, and Bob headed for his car, pleased that this night, there was no one waiting to try and kill him. He stopped at the local 7-Eleven and bought a paper so he could read the engagement announcement.

CHAPTER 18

THE TIN MAN AND TESTIMONIES

At the same time Bob, Betty, and Cindy were having dinner at Betty's apartment, the Tin Man was sequestered in his rented room in Sugar Land, Texas. He had bought a pepperoni pizza at Pizza Hut and was halfway through it. On the table in front of him, he had a copy of the *Houston Chronicle* spread out. It was turned to the Weddings and Engagements page. Because he had been shadowing Bob Graver on an irregular basis, he suspected that the relationship with the police lieutenant was getting serious. So he had been monitoring the paper. He was constantly looking for opportunities to eliminate the only eyewitness to his Massey Chemical plant arson. There was no date published for the wedding, but it mentioned that it would be held some time in December at the Faith Community Church in Deer Park.

Although arsonists are not known for their honesty, the Tin Man was bothered by the fact that he had accepted money to hire a hit man to take out Garver and his girlfriend, the policewoman. John Swisher had been bugging him on the new burner phone about either returning the money or executing the hit. Apparently, Swisher had been interviewed by the police, and he was scared stiff. He was beginning to bug the Tin Man so much that he was seriously starting to think about changing the target of his hit to Swisher. The Tin Man had given Penny Lusher, the hit woman, $25,000 for the hit, a rather cheap price for two murders. He now thought that he should probably have spent more for someone competent.

The hit had gone bad, and Lusher had gone belly-up in the restaurant, leaving her quarries upright and breathing. She had also been dumb enough to carry the $25,000 with her, so the police recovered it, deducing that it had been a hit. From the Tin Man's perspective, Lusher's immediate death was fortunate, since she could not tie the Tin Man into the hit. But strangely enough, he felt guilty about having accepted Swisher's $50,000 and not providing the service that he offered. He decided, *"If you want something done right, do it yourself."* And he began planning Bob Garver's demise.

The activities surrounding the upcoming wedding should provide cover, and people would be focused on those activities rather than suspecting an attack. Bachelor parties were typically crazy events, and thus unpredictable. Although Garver would obviously be in attendance, it wasn't long in his thoughts because it was hard to find out the details of when and where, and it was too unpredictable. Some families of the groom threw a dinner prior to the wedding—that might be an opportunity. But if all else failed, the hit could take place at the wedding ceremony itself; obviously, the victim would be there, out in the open. He had learned that Garver and his girlfriend regularly attended the Faith Community Church in Deer Park. He planned to visit to get the layout of the church so his plans would reflect reality. He also planned to attend a couple of other weddings at the church to understand the normal procedure. With that decided, he polished off the rest of the pepperoni pizza and went to bed, sleeping like a baby.

The next morning at work, Bob Garver gave Pastor Don Lancy a call. He explained that he had been attending for a couple of months and wanted to join the church. He mentioned that he was the guy that had been sitting next to Betty Marcum in the services. Don said he knew who he was and apologized that they had not met formally. He noted that in a large church like Faith Community, there were so many people to greet as they left the service, that there just was not time to talk in depth with anyone. Bob said he understood. Don explained that to join their church, it was necessary to be interviewed by the elder board and to tell them how you had accepted Christ. Bob said this was no problem and asked when he could meet with them. Don said that he would arrange for the interview this coming Sunday after the service.

Bob then explained that he and Betty had discussed the need for premarital counseling and that another member, Cindy Parker, had said that Don was qualified to give that counseling. He wondered if Don would be available on Sunday evening, since Betty's police work was hard to schedule around. Don said that would be fine and suggested they meet at 7:30 p.m. on Sunday, a week after the interview with the elders. Bob thought that would be fine, but said he would confirm it with Betty. Don said he appreciated them approaching him for this— he said most couples never get any premarital counselling at all. Bob complimented Don on his verse-by-verse preaching of the Bible and said that he had learned quite a bit since attending. Don thanked him, confirmed the counselling appointment, and they hung up. Bob thought, *"That went well, I really like that guy."*

Bob made a quick call to Betty to make sure the date and time for the counselling was okay. It was. He told her that he would be interviewed by the elders this upcoming Sunday and asked her to pray that it would go okay. She said that she had been interviewed about two years ago, and there was nothing to it. You just had to give your testimony about how you accepted Jesus as Savior.

She said, *"In fact, I know you are a Christian, but I've never heard how you became one. Maybe next time we meet you can use me to practice on."*

Bob said, *"No problem, I enjoy telling people about it. And maybe you can tell me about your experience too."*

They agreed to meet for dinner at Denny's and cover this important topic.

At 5:00 p.m., Bob pulled into the Denny's parking lot. Betty's car was not there, so he listened to country music on the radio until she arrived. They walked into Denny's hand in hand, and Betty asked for a table facing the entrance. This was getting to be a habit for both of them. Betty ordered a Bourbon Sizzlin' Skillet consisting of two seasoned chicken breasts covered with a bourbon glaze, topped with roasted bell peppers, onions, and mushrooms—all atop broccoli and seasoned red-skinned potatoes. A fairly healthy meal. On the other hand, Bob ordered seasoned meatballs atop a bed of pasta covered in tomato sauce and served with a side of Italian cheeses. He would have to increase his jogging distance tomorrow to make up for it.

While they waited for their meals, Bob told Betty how he had accepted Christ.

"As a teenager, I had always thought about God, but the church my parents attended had never made the gospel clear—or at least I had never heard and understood it. However, the church youth group was going to attend a youth rally at a local high school, and I decided to go with them. The speaker at the rally was a Methodist bishop, whose message was very simple. He presented it as bad news followed by good news. He said the bad news is that we are all sinners, which means we have fallen short of God's perfection. He included himself—no one met God's requirement of holiness. He quoted the Bible, 'The wages of sin is death,' and explained that was spiritual death and separation from God in hell. I was sitting there thinking, 'But I've been a pretty good guy—maybe God will take that into account.' Then the bishop killed that idea by quoting the Old Testament, 'All our righteous deeds are like filthy rags.' God sees even our best efforts as worthless. He pounded it home with more Bible verses: 'There is none righteous, not even one; there is none who understands, there is none who seeks for God; all have turned aside, together they have become useless; there is none who does good, there is not even one.'

"I sat there thinking to myself, 'Then there is no hope for anyone!' But then the bishop dropped the good news (gospel) on us. He said that even though there is nothing I can do to satisfy God's requirement for perfection, and I deserve eternal death because of it, there is someone who has satisfied God's requirement for perfection—Jesus Christ. He explained how in the Old Testament the priest would kill an animal sacrifice and pour its blood on the altar, which protected Israel from God's judgment of their sins. But he explained that this was only a symbol—pointing forward to the time when the perfect sacrifice would shed His blood for the sins of the entire world. He said that Jesus was the perfect sacrifice (He was called the Lamb of God). When He died on the cross, He paid the penalty for the sin that we all owe. We couldn't do anything to earn our salvation, so He did it for us. The bishop said that one way to look at it was that every one of our sins—past, present, and future—were placed on the sinless Lamb of God as He died on the cross. We deserved that death—but He died in our place.

"Wow! That was good news to me. I wanted to stand up and ask the bishop, 'Why would He do that for me!' But he explained it simply. Christ died for you—because He loves you. That hit me like a ton of bricks! He loves me? Then the bishop explained that Christ had provided the way to heaven as a free gift—there was nothing anyone could do to earn it. He said that the only way you can acquire a free gift is to accept it by faith. He

*asked if there was anyone in the audience that wanted to accept that gift,
and invited us to come to the front. I was out of my seat and running down
the aisle of the stadium to stand in front of him.*

*"He asked us to pray a simple prayer. 'Dear Lord, I am a sinner. Your
Bible tells me that because of that, I am destined for hell. I realize there
is nothing I can do in my own power to change that and make myself
acceptable in Your sight. But I've learned tonight that Jesus has paid the
penalty for my sin on the cross. He died for me, He rose again from the
grave, and He is seated in heaven today. Dear Lord, I accept what You did
for me on the cross, I believe You have paid the price for my sins, I want
You to take over my life and save me from judgment. Thank You, Lord,
for saving my soul.'*

*"That was it! They gave each of us a silver necklace, with a cross on it,
to remind us of what had happened. But the necklace wasn't necessary—I
would never be the same. I had confidence in my eternal destiny with Him.
I have not always been the best of Christians, but with His salvation, I am
eternally secure. And He has always been there when I need Him."*

Betty's eyes were filled with tears. She said, *"Thank you for telling
that to me, Bob. I knew you were a Christian, but that is a wonderful
testimony."* She said that her testimony wasn't all that dramatic, because
she had accepted Christ as an eight-year-old child in Sunday school.

She said, *"I remember my teacher telling the class Bible stories each
week, and she always ended the class by asking if anyone wanted to accept
Jesus as their Savior. One Sunday, I did just that, and I have never regretted
the decision."*

Bob said, *"Don't knock it, that's a fine testimony, Betty. As a young
girl, you simply accepted what Christ has done for you. Your sins are
forgiven, and you have eternal life. You can't beat that!"*

Bob told Betty that he had a lot of growing to do following salvation.
And one reason was that there was no one to mentor him. For example,
he had a big issue accepting that the Bible was God's word. After all,
he reasoned, it was written by men, so it must be filled with errors.
He started attending a different church that taught the Bible, and was
elected as a deacon. He frequently got into discussions (arguments?)
about the Bible with one particular deacon. Becoming frustrated, this
deacon said, *"Bob, you're ignorant! You keep questioning the validity of
the Bible, but you haven't even read it! That's dumb!"*

Bob told Betty, *"Well—that made me angry—so I went out and got a Halley's Bible Handbook and began to read the Bible along with Halley's starting with Genesis 1:1. I wouldn't recommend that sequence, but that's what I did. By the time I had finished Revelation, I knew this was the Word of God. Yes, it had multiple authors, but it was one story. Mistakes? Errors? I found none—there were difficult passages, but they had reasonable explanations given by reasonable men. To this day, I thank God for sending that guy into my life to call me dumb! Because, indeed, I was."*

Again, Betty's eyes were teared up. The waitress gave her a strange look as she gave them their dinners. Their dinners were very tasty, and Bob gave the waitress an extra big tip. He followed Betty home to her apartment, primarily to give her a good night kiss. Tomorrow was another day, and Betty planned to call her mother to coordinate some of the wedding issues, like the guest list. Bob was glad that he wouldn't be involved, other than giving Betty his list of guests.

CHAPTER 19

THE NET CLOSES

John Swisher sat in his office on the thirtieth floor of Massey Tower. He was staring out the window at the marvelous view, which normally he admired because it made him feel important. After all, he had risen from a lowly engineer at one of the less-important plants to the esteemed position of vice president of operations. He didn't like to think about some of the underhanded methods he had used to get him the promotions. He was now over all of Massey's operating plants. But today, the great view of Houston did not inspire him.

That speck of dirt, Bob Garver, had the gall to get the police to question him about the Deer Park fires. And when confronted in the eleventh floor engineering meeting, he had stood up to him! He was going to wish he had never been born! Swisher had attempted to get Garver fired, but it appeared that Garver had friends in high places. Garver's immediate boss, Ralph Swenson, had essentially thrown him out of the meeting—he would regret that. Later he had talked with the vice president of Engineering to get them both fired. He was told to "play in his own playpen" and stay out of theirs. How humiliating. He would make them pay for it, if it took him the rest of his career. He had tried complaining to the president of Massey and received no support at all. How was he expected to function, surrounded by all these incompetent jerks?

And to top it all off, that snotty police lieutenant had essentially accused him of hiring the arsonist. Of course, he had, but her attitude showed no respect. He had acquired a few acquaintances in the underworld because he liked to gamble. It was amazing who you got to know when you played poker with the big boys. That was how he got the name of Marcus Stalinbeck, the arsonist. He was highly recommended by a union boss in one of the games. But he had sure turned out to be a big disappointment. That snoop Garver had seen him by chance at the time of the first fire. Originally, Stalinbeck had decided to "do it himself" and bump off the witness.

Swisher couldn't blame him for wanting to kill Garver; he would like to do that himself. But he was starting to question Stalinbeck's competence. First, he messed up a knife attack, finding out too late that Garver carried a concealed weapon. Then, in following Garver, he had been discovered, and had his picture taken. Dumb! He was almost killed when he attempted to shoot Garver during a car chase. He was messing things up so badly that Swisher contacted him on the burner phone and told him that he would pay for a different hit man to dispose of Garver. He also told Stalinbeck that he had better not tie him back to the crimes. It wasn't cheap nowadays to hire a hit man—$50,000. He knew the US Government watched money transfers over $10,000, so he made ten withdrawals of $5,000 each and did a dead drop to pass the money to Stalinbeck. A dead drop is a method of spy tradecraft used to pass items or information between two individuals using a secret location. By avoiding direct meetings, they keep anyone from finding out they knew one another. He thought he was being so clever.

But Swisher thought the idiot arsonist hired a female hit man, and she managed to get herself killed during the hit. Incredible bad luck! What's worse, he thought, she had her cell phone with her, and it linked her to the arsonist's burner phone. By combining that information with the fact that he had also called the burner phone, they began to suspect him even more. The result was the police interview in his office at Massey Tower. He had tolerated the rudeness for a while, but then told the lady police officer to get out—he would not answer any more questions without his lawyer present. That had certainly not reduced her suspicion that he was involved. He discussed his problem with a defense attorney who told him that they obviously did not have a case against him—it is not illegal to make a phone call, even if it is to a suspect's phone. There were all kinds of legal defenses against that kind of charge. The lawyer recommended he forget the whole thing unless the police came back.

Suddenly, his secretary buzzed him and said that a Lieutenant Betty Marcum from the Deer Park Police was in the outer office.

He said, *"Tell her that I'm busy and that I need my lawyer present for any meetings."*

His secretary buzzed back after a minute and said, *"She says that unless you talk with her, she will be back with a warrant for your arrest."*

Swisher said, *"Send her in."*

Lieutenant Betty Marcum was loaded for bear, and she noted that Swisher's face was red as a beet. He was obviously flustered.

She said, *"We have made several discoveries regarding your finances that need to be explained."*

He said, *"I don't want to answer any questions without my lawyer present."*

Betty said, *"Okay, we'll do this at police headquarters after I get the warrant and arrest you. Why don't you make this easy on yourself and answer a few questions?"*

Swisher could see this quickly getting out of control, so he agreed to let her ask the questions.

"Why do you need an offshore account in the Cayman Islands?"

Swisher answered, *"It's not illegal to have an offshore account. There are tax advantages that you poor people wouldn't understand."*

Betty asked, *"How do you account for the large money transfers into that account following each of the Deer Park fires and explosion?"*

Swisher said, *"I don't have to explain any transfers. That is none of your business. And I find it offensive that you have spied on my financial affairs. My lawyer will be filing suit."*

Betty replied, *"We had a warrant, go ahead and sue. But you haven't answered my question—where did the large money transfers come from?"*

Swisher said, *"I made some good investments."*

Betty replied, *"You sure did! You did short sales on Massey stock just before the fires and explosion. That's wonderful—you must have a great fortune-teller! And by the way, we have informed the Securities and Exchange Commission that they might want to investigate your 'luck.'"*

Swisher's face was so red that Betty thought he might explode.

He said, *"I think this meeting is over!"*

Betty replied, *"Okay, but tying all this to the fact that you called a burner phone that has been linked to an arsonist and that you can't explain where the $50,000 withdrawal went—oh, didn't I tell you that we know about that too?—and that within forty-eight hours of the withdrawal, a murder attempt was made on the arson prime witness. Well, you can draw your own conclusions. This meeting may be over, but rest assured, we will be back."*

Betty walked quickly out of Swisher's office.

His secretary asked, *"What's going on? Is John going to be arrested?"*

Betty replied, *"Not today—but if I were you, I would be looking for a job transfer to another boss."*

In the background, Betty heard Swisher pounding on his desk. He was shouting into the phone that his lawyer better d*** well call him back immediately. Betty thought, *Objective achieved—upset people make mistakes.*

And that is exactly what John Swisher did. He called the arsonist on his new burner phone. He told him that the police were on his tail and that he needed to get the witness, Bob Garver, killed right away.

He said, *"How could you hire someone that stupid for the hit? She didn't even get a shot off! What good are you?"*

The arsonist Steinbeck yelled back at him, telling him he was stupid to call him on that phone. He said he would throw it away later and call him on a new burner phone with another number.

He told Swisher that he already had plans to get rid of Garver at an event he would be attending in the next few weeks. Swisher offered him another $5,000 incentive to be paid after Garver was dead. What neither of them knew was that, in accordance with a warrant, Mack the Hack (Mack Turner—Deer Park Police) was monitoring the call in a police van parked by Massey Tower, and he quickly found the arsonist's location. He was in the Marriott Hotel in Sugar Land, Texas. Most importantly, they had John Swisher essentially confessing to the upcoming hit on Bob Garver, and by implication, to the hit at the Shrimp Galore restaurant.

Betty called her dispatcher and asked him to get the Sugar Land police to make the arrest. She also dispatched two Deer Park police officers to the Sugar Land location to provide backup. Unfortunately, the dispatcher ran into some political stonewalling, and it took the Sugar Land police over an hour to get to the address. It is about an hour from Deer Park to Sugar Land, and the Deer Park police arrived slightly before the Sugar Land police. By the time they all arrived, Stalinbeck was gone. He was obviously a smart, cautious person. The hotel said that he paid in cash and cleared out. They confirmed that it was the arsonist by looking at the photographs. From now on, Mack the Hack would be monitoring Swisher's office, home, and cell phones to get the arsonist's new burner phone number. Betty was a bit disappointed, but the net was closing.

CHAPTER 20

COUNSELING

Bob picked Betty up at 7:00 p.m. on Sunday, and they headed for the Faith Community Church for their first premarital counseling session. Don Lancy, the pastor, met them as they were coming into the office area. He had made coffee and brought some Krispy Kreme donuts to eat. The donuts won Bob to his side right away!

He said, *"There's nothing like a Krispy Kreme donut! I love 'em."*

They went into the pastor's office and settled down for the session. Bob and Betty sat together on the couch, and the pastor sat across from them in a living room–type chair.

Don started the meeting with prayer for Bob and Betty and asked God's blessing upon their upcoming marriage. He asked for God's guidance as they discussed marriage and their relationship. He then commented, *"By the time you decide to get engaged, you probably know each other pretty well. You know the quirks, pet peeves, and favorite kind of pizza. You are also, obviously, thinking that this is the person you want to spend the rest of your life with. So you might ask, 'What good will premarital counseling do?' It turns out that this type of counseling gives you a safe space to explore what you expect from the relationship and how to handle those expectations now and later. I've found that there are a number of thought-provoking questions that help in premarital counseling. First, do you have any questions?"* Pause. *"If not, let's get started.*

"First question, have you discussed how many children you want?"

Bob said, *"Betty and I have discussed this, and we are initially thinking two or three."*

Betty agreed, then said, *"Two would be fine if we had a boy and a girl. But three in case we don't."*

Don said, *"It's quite a while until it happens—I hope, but you both have jobs, how would you care for them?"*

Betty said, *"Our jobs are quite important to us. But I would take several months off after each birth to establish a firm relationship with the child. The police department allows that. On the other hand, I think we would hire a nanny for the preschool years."*

Bob agreed.

Don asked about their schooling.

Bob said, *"With the way public schools are teaching the kids low moral values, I would hope to afford a private Christian academy."*

Betty agreed.

Don asked, *"Regarding discipline, would you be stern or lax?"*

Bob answered, *"I believe the Bible advocates 'Spare the rod and spoil the child.' I believe sometimes strong discipline is required. But it always should be followed by showing the child that you love them and that it was their behavior that was not acceptable, that they are always accepted."*

Betty liked that answer and added, *"I have seen what lack of discipline has done to teenagers that I have had to arrest. The Bible knows what it is talking about!"*

Don said, *"I normally ask about differences in religion, but you two have both given your testimonies to our elders and have shown me already that Christ is important to you. Do you see any problems in that area?"*

Bob said, *"With the Word of God as our foundation, it is unlikely that we will run into religious differences that would cause problems."*

Betty agreed.

Don said, *"The next area causes more problems than most others— money! First, how much do you each expect to contribute to the household?"*

Betty said, *"We both make about the same amount, so initially there won't be that kind of competition. Neither of us has accumulated any debt, so that won't be a problem. I believe finances should start by giving at least 10 percent to the church. I don't believe in tithing, that is an Old Testament law concept, but it seems like a reasonable amount since God has given us everything we have. I also think we should try to save another 10 percent, but that is not rigid. I believe we should combine our finances—joint accounts—and make decisions together when large purchases are involved."*

Bob added, *"To start with, for normal household purchases—food, gasoline, etc.—I would like to use what I call an 'envelope system.' At the beginning of each month, we would place the allotted amount of cash in its own envelope. When the money runs out, we would either stop spending for that commodity or move money from some other envelope. Once that kind of budget is established for a time, it can be relaxed when both of us are used to the new situation. Emergency expenses would normally be handled out of the 10 percent savings. My father taught me that there are only two things you should borrow for—a house and a car. I think he was right. Everything else can come out of savings.*

"But I have found a better idea that I have called the Fund. Everyone has annual expenses—insurance, taxes, etc. I total all of those annual amounts, divide by twelve, and make sure that I put that amount into the Fund every month. Then when an annual expense pops up—it is not an emergency, because the money is already there.

Betty commented, *"Wow! You have put a lot of thought into this. Let's begin using your envelope system and the Fund to get our finances established.*

"But I would like to have some money that I can call 'my own' to buy gifts etc."

Bob said, *"I can understand that. Let's discuss the amount, and you can treat it as your own—you can spend it as you wish."*

Don said, *"You seem to be better prepared on the subject of money than most couples.*

"The next subject competes with money for the top problem spot. Can you guess what it is?"

Bob said, *"Sex."*

Don replied, *"You win! How important is sex to you, and how much sex do you envision having?"*

Betty said, *"Wow! You don't pull any punches, do you? I guess that I have observed that sex seems more important to men than to women. As a policewoman, that may be based on not seeing many men who are raped by women. I think women are more focused on the romance and intimacy than they are on the act itself."*

Bob commented, *"Men and women are certainly different—that shows I'm a master of understatement. But I have to tell you that sex is extremely important to me, and most men. Just look at the number of TV commercials you see for erectile dysfunction. I expect that we will have sex quite frequently at the start (for example on our honeymoon), but that it will taper off to about once a week."*

Betty said, *"I can live with that. And we need to be open enough to talk about our likes and dislikes. But remember that my greatest pleasure is not the act itself, but the romance leading up to the act."*

Bob said, *"I can live with that, too."*

Don next asked, *"Where will you live?"*

Betty answered, *"We've discussed that, and because I have an apartment roommate, I will initially move in with Bob. But I would hope that after a few years, we could buy a house and start a family."*

Bob said, *"Sounds right to me."*

Don then asked, *"How will you spend your weekends and vacations?"*

Bob said, *"It think we are basically stay-at-home folks. I don't believe we need to be entertained every weekend. However, a few weekends a year, I would hope to take short trips to see some of Texas. We would discuss and plan it ahead of time. I'm sure some vacation time would be spent visiting relatives, but I think we both have bucket lists of places we would like to save for and travel to."*

Betty was pretty much in agreement.

Don next asked, *"Who is going to do the household chores—clothes washing, dishwashing, cleaning, etc.?"*

Betty answered, *"I would hope that some can be done together, like dishwashing. But the rest we can discuss, and I would hope that we would share the load."*

Bob said, *"I am willing to do it all. But I'm convinced that she feels the same way, and I don't expect any real problems in that area."*

Don said, *"Last question. When, not if, you have disagreements, how will you resolve them?"*

Bob answered, *"I tend to clam up, so I will have to make an extra effort to talk out our problems."*

Betty said, *"My problem is I lean toward blaming others for conflict. I will have to fight that. And discussing the issue, without accusing anyone, should help."*

Don commented, *"I'm impressed with how much thought you two have given this. I fully expect it to be a long, wonderful, and Christ-controlled marriage."*

Don closed the meeting with prayer. Bob and Betty left the meeting feeling pretty good about their ability to get along after marriage. They agreed that it would take work, but that it was worth the effort—and that the fact that they were very much in love would help them get over any problems.

CHAPTER 21

WEDDING PLANS

Betty had asked her mother, Marsha Marcum, to come down to Deer Park from Cleveland, Texas, to plan the details of the wedding. She arrived on Tuesday at 10:00 a.m. and couldn't stop talking about the horrible traffic coming down the Eastex Freeway and through town. Betty suggested that next time she should try coming around the east Beltway, which should have less traffic. Betty served a brunch, consisting of cinnamon buns and coffee, which helped her mother to calm down a bit. They brought each other up to date on their lives before diving into the wedding plans. Since Betty's apartment had a guest bedroom, her mother planned to stay for a couple of weeks to help coordinate the wedding.

Marsha said, *"Betty, your father has been saving money for years, looking forward to your wedding. Anything you want, he will pay for."*

It was tradition for the father of the bride to pay for the wedding, perhaps going way back to the presentation of a dowry. The fact that money was not an issue relieved much of the tension that can occur over wedding expenses.

Marsha said, *"Betty, just have fun with this—money is not a problem."*

The first issue they addressed was the participants—for example, how many bridesmaids and who the maid of honor would be.

Betty said, *"I want Cindy Parker to be my maid of honor. I have roomed with her for several years, and I've grown quite close to her."*

Since Betty had graduated from a local high school, and was working locally, she said she would select four of her former classmates that she kept in touch with on a regular basis. She had discussed this with Bob Garver, and he had said he would like Ralph Swenson (his head office boss) as his best man, since they went way back to the time when he made sales calls on him at the Massey Plant in New Jersey. Bob's four groomsmen would be Frank Baron (who had retired) and Fred Conway, Jack Fishbane, and Harold Neymeir from the olefins plant start-up team.

Marsha said, *"It's wonderful that you and Bob have done this much planning. But it is important that you begin to get confirmation from them. To do that, you will need to settle on a firm date for the wedding."*

They looked at a calendar and selected Saturday, December fifteenth—ten days before Christmas.

The next item they discussed was where the wedding would be held.

Betty said, *"We both want it to be at the Faith Community Church in Deer Park, where we are both members. I will ask Pastor Lancy to reserve December 15 and perform the ceremony. The church is blessed with a fantastic organist and pianist, so I will try and confirm that they are available on the fifteenth for the pre-ceremony music and, of course, the wedding processional and recessional."*

Marsha said, *"Your father will give the pastor a check for $1,000 and each of the two musicians $500 checks. He has asked around and thinks these figures are generous. Do you agree?"*

Betty said, *"I don't know. Dad's the expert. It seems like too much to me. But I expect that will make it super easy for me to get their commitments!"*

Although specific close friends in the church would receive invitations, Betty said, *"The marriage will also be announced from the pulpit, stating that everyone is invited to the wedding and to the reception following. That will add to the cost of the reception, but I am relying on Dad's directions regarding funds."*

This would also make the reception cost more difficult to predict, but they would estimate on the high side.

Marsha had some graphics design training and had worked up a wedding invitation for Betty's approval. On the outside it featured a little boy and girl, about five years old, dressed up in wedding clothes, marching down the aisle. As the invitation was opened, on the left side would be up-to-date pictures of Betty and Bob (photos to be taken).

Information regarding the date, time, etc. would be on the right side. Betty loved the design. Marsha had made a first attempt at the invitation wording, but they now worked on it and finalized the information.

At her mother's suggestion, Betty had arranged to meet with a wedding coordinator to discuss the wedding dress and bridesmaids' dresses that day at 2:00 p.m. in downtown Houston. Once the dresses were selected, the same supplier would also handle the men's attire, so Bob Garver was to join them around 3:30 p.m. The church had held many weddings during the years; in fact, there were two weddings scheduled prior to this one. The church had multiple wedding decorations stored in their attic that could be used. Betty agreed to ask the person in the church who handled decorations if she would decorate the church and coordinate this with the deacons. This woman loved to decorate, but Betty's father would give her a check for $500 for any incidental expenses. This was added to the to-do list that they had begun to develop.

Betty said, *"I had no idea that planning a wedding was such a big project! Thanks, Mom, for taking on this task—I really appreciate it!"*

The wedding reception following the service was a huge task, and Marsha suggested that she take this on since Betty was a police lieutenant and had less time to work on it. They would also pay the wedding coordinator to make sure everything went well during the wedding and reception, since she would be otherwise occupied with mother-of-the-bride issues.

Marsha's and the coordinator's first task would be to evaluate local caterers and then find a small ensemble to supply the music. The coordinator would also order and time the arrival of the flowers for the wedding and the reception. The coordinator's experience should provide some good ideas about these functions. Betty had asked the pastor if there was any prohibition regarding dancing. He said there was not and cited David's dancing before the Ark of the Covenant in 2 Samuel 6:13–14—but he would clear it with the elders and expected no issues. That would influence the selection of the musical ensemble.

Betty's mother said, *"Since money is not an issue, for the reception, I would like to have a full meal in the church fellowship hall."*

Betty commented, *"I will coordinate that with the church deacons regarding setup and take down of the tables and chairs."*

She would offer Bob Garver's help in the setup (he would be otherwise occupied on their honeymoon during the takedown time). Since the deacons would not accept monetary payment, she would offer to donate $1,000 (of Daddy's money) to the building fund in their names.

This caused Betty and her mother to think about a master of ceremonies to coordinate the reception activities following the meal. There would be the opening prayer, the introduction of the bride and groom, and their first dance. The parents of the bride must have a dance, followed by the parents of the groom. The best man would need to make a toast, and there might be other people who wished to say a few words.

Betty said, *"I'll see if Bob will ask his best man, Ralph Swenson, to be master of ceremonies."*

Marsha said, *"You know, it would be easier to coordinate everything if the wedding party is put up in a local hotel, close to the church, the night before the wedding. Your dad will pay for it. That will assure that everyone is there and gets to the wedding on time."* Marsha also indicated that Betty's father would pay for the wedding party's dinner in the hotel restaurant the night before the wedding. Although that was traditionally the family of the groom's responsibility, with Bob's parents living in upstate New York, that would make it difficult to coordinate. Following the dinner, this situation would also make the bachelor's party much easier for Bob's best man to coordinate, since all the guys would be in one place.

Betty agreed with this strategy, and Marsha said, *"I will make the hotel and restaurant reservations. I'll also take on the task of arranging for limousines to carry the wedding party to the church and for the limousine to take you and Bob to your honeymoon suite at the hotel. They will also pick you up the next morning to take you to the airport."*

Betty indicated that she and Bob would make sure everyone "bought into" the idea of staying in a local hotel the night before the wedding—it was free—why not? Marsha would also update her husband, John, about all these plans—and if he lived through the shock, they would proceed.

The mention of the honeymoon caused Marsha to ask Betty if they had thought about where they wanted to go. Oddly enough, Betty and Bob had not decided. They added it to the to-do list to talk with Bob about the honeymoon that afternoon. Again, Marsha assured Betty that her father would be footing the bill. They made a list of possible destinations to promote discussion: Hawaii, Jamaica, Europe, New Zealand, and a few others. Honeymoon tickets and hotel reservations were added to the to-do list.

Time was flying by, and it was lunchtime, so Betty took her mother to Las Hadas Mexican Restaurant in Deer Park, where they shared an order of fajitas. Then, it was time to drive to downtown Houston to meet with the wedding coordinator.

They began the meeting with the wedding coordinator, Linda Marker, by going over the multitude of items that had been discussed that morning. She was impressed with the amount of thought that had already gone into the planning. The coordinator showed them about a thousand wedding dresses, and after much debate, an off-shoulder, lace-sleeved tulle ballgown wedding dress was selected, having a huge flowing train. This would necessitate having a young girl to help with the train as Betty moved from one place to another.

They had forgotten that they needed a flower girl to scatter flower petals down the aisle.

Betty had a cool idea; she said, *"I know two young twins in our church who could serve both functions. One could be the flower girl, and the other would help with the wedding dress train. I will see if their parents will let them do it."*

Betty then selected light-blue bridesmaid convertible infinity dresses with a wrap design that could accommodate different sizes. A white plumeria lei crown would adorn each woman's hair. The twins would have matching outfits.

Linda Marker had several caterers that she had used in the past, and she had actually coordinated two weddings at the Faith Community Church in Deer Park—that was a plus. They discussed what type of cuisine they wanted. Betty had no big preference but said that they were pretty basic people, and it should not be too fancy.

She said, *"It would be nice if we could pronounce it."*

They all laughed, and Linda said she knew what she meant. She suggested they discuss it with Bob when he arrived at 3:30 p.m.

They discussed what kind of music the ensemble should play for dinner and dancing. Betty said that both she and Bob were old enough that the modern hard-rock stuff turned them off. It would be nice if during dinner the music was mainly light classical.

During the dancing, she preferred *"to actually dance touching my partner, not to use it as an excuse to throw a physical fit."*

Linda again said she understood and that there were a couple of ensembles that they might want to go see before selecting one.

Bob arrived promptly at 3:30 p.m. and was introduced to Linda Marker. She showed Bob the wedding dress that Betty had selected—he was blown away.

He said, *"Betty, you always look beautiful, but in that dress, you will cause the men's hearts to go into cardiac arrest!"*

She replied, *"Aw, shucks, Gomer! You say the sweetest thangs!"*

Everybody had a good laugh. Linda showed him the light-blue bridesmaid's dresses with the white plumeria hair crowns. He thought they were gorgeous.

Then the topic turned to the men's wedding attire. Bob said that he didn't really care—anything Betty picked would be fine with him.

Betty said, *"Since this is a December wedding, I suggest that the men wear conventional black tuxedos with red-and-green bow ties."*

Linda and Marsha liked the idea, and it caused them to suggest that the reception decorations and flowers might have a Christmas theme.

Bob added, *"Let's make sure the decorations reflect the birth of Jesus in some way."*

Betty agreed. Linda didn't think that would be any problem.

Betty told Linda that with her full-time police job, she would not always be available for answers. She said that she had appointed her mother, Marsha, with full authority to make decisions on her behalf. Linda commented that would make her life much easier. Marsha commented that she had been working the details regarding the hotel, limousines, etc., but that she would be more than happy to turn those details over to Linda. That was fine with Linda, since it put the total responsibility in one place. She indicated that she would plan to visit with Marsha in the next few days to receive any information she had already gathered. They could also visit the hotel to look at their facilities and discuss the events with the manager.

Bob was asked about what food should be the main course at the reception. Again, he had no preference, but backed up Betty's comment that they were "simple folk," so Linda should not select anything "weird." Since neither one of the couple had a preference, Linda suggested broiled Alaska salmon. They both liked that, but Betty reminded Linda that someone might have an allergy to seafood. Linda said that the caterer would have a second choice available for anyone with that problem. They would use a buffet line to eliminate the need for many waiters and reduce the time needed to serve the dinner. A few hired waiters would circulate among the tables filling water glasses and removing dishes when needed. They would also bring out the desserts on trays so a second buffet line was not needed.

Bob said, *"It sounds like mass confusion to me—I'm glad you ladies are handling it. I'm sure it will be fabulous!"*

They then discussed where to go on the honeymoon.

Bob joked, *"It doesn't matter, we'll only see the inside of the hotel room."*

After the ladies put on "I'm shocked" looks, Linda brought out the list of possible destinations they had thrown together that morning. Almost immediately, Bob and Betty were sold on Hawaii. Bob had done some research and thought the islands of Kawaii and Hawaii (the Big Island) offered lots to see. Since Betty had no island preference, they agreed to honeymoon on those two islands. Linda would make the airline and hotel reservations as well as scheduling a couple of interesting tours.

Everybody agreed it had been a beneficial meeting. Linda said she would work up an estimate and email it to Marsha, suggesting that she "prepare" her husband for a shock. Everyone laughed but Bob; he smiled, but he was thinking about the next time he would meet John Marcum—would John have a new name for him?—"Big Spender!" He had not been in the early discussion about how Betty's father told her to do whatever she wanted for her wedding, that cost was not to be considered. Bob had taken on a new task—getting buy-in from the men he wanted for his best man and groomsmen, including their staying at the local hotel the night before the wedding. The fact that Betty's father was paying for everything would certainly make it easier to get their commitment. And he had to get his best man, Ralph Swenson, to be master of ceremonies at the reception, give the toast to the bride and groom, and plan the bachelor's party—warning him to keep the bachelor's party within the bounds of decency.

CHAPTER 22

THE GROOMSMEN

Believe it or not, the olefins plant was up and running. The plant was approaching its design rate of 2 billion pounds/year of ethylene. There had been no fires of explosions during the latest start-up. Operations management was happy, and all was well in the Massey Chemical world. And best of all, the Tin Man had not tried killing Bob Garver in weeks! He was beginning to think his luck had changed. If this kept up, he might even stop carrying his 9 mm pistol to and from Massey. Work for the instrument engineers was moving from troubleshooting start-up problems to handling small projects where potential improvements had been discovered during the start-up.

Bob called Ralph Swenson as soon as head office opened at 8:00 a.m. He wanted to make sure he would agree to be his best man.

After the usual small talk, Bob said, *"Ralph, I wanted to let you know that Betty and I will be getting married on December 15. Can you make it?"*

Ralph said that he sure would.

Then Bob dropped the bomb. *"Ralph, I would appreciate it if you would be my best man. You and I go back many years to the New Jersey plant, and I can't think of anyone I would rather have as my best man. You were a great customer, have been a great boss, and you've been a great friend—okay, have I buttered you up enough?"*

Ralph said, *"You want me as best man? But that will confirm what everyone already knows! I am!"*

Laughter on both ends. *"Sure, I will be your best man. What does it involve?"*

Bob said, *"Not much. As the musical lyrics go, 'Get me to the church on time!' You will need to stand next to me during the service and keep me from fainting. If I forget my line, 'I do,' you need to punch me and remind me. Then you need to hand me the wedding ring without dropping it. Sound too complex for you? But seriously, you will also need to be the master of ceremonies at the reception, give a toast to the bride and groom, and most importantly, you will need to organize a bachelor party that doesn't soil my reputation."*

Ralph replied, *"Soil your reputation, what reputation? Sure, I'll be glad to handle all those details, and I'll make sure you don't back out at the last minute!"*

Laughter on both ends.

Bob said, *"You will get an official invitation by snail mail that gives the time and place. And by the way, the father of the bride is paying for the 'uniforms'—tuxedos. And he is also paying for the bachelor party and for the entire wedding party to stay at the Holiday Inn Express & Suites in Deer Park the night before the wedding—suites for everyone, of course)."* He joked, *"You can bring your wife or that hussy you are running around with. Tell her there is a dinner the night before the wedding—maybe that will help get her to come—free food!*

"Everyone in the same hotel will make it easier for you to organize the bachelor party since all of the men should be staying there. A limousine will take you and the wedding party to the church and return you after the reception. We thought that would be wise. Otherwise, it might resemble herding cats!"

Ralph said, *"And we might have trouble finding our cars after the wild bachelor party I'm going to throw!"*

Bob replied, *"Ralph, you remember not to go crazy with this! And thanks for volunteering to do this!"*

Following the phone call with Ralph Swenson, Bob walked down the hall of the start-up trailer. He found Jack Fishbane and Fred Conway in Jack's office.

"Hey, guys, I need a favor. It would be wonderful if you two would be groomsmen in my wedding on December 15. Your tuxedos are paid for, so there wouldn't be any expense. And something unusual, Betty's father is paying for a hotel suite for each of you the night before, to make getting

everyone to the church on time easier. And if you wish, your wives stay at the hotel with you. Can I count on you?"

Both men said they would be glad to.

Then Jack said, *"Congratulations, you lucky dog, but Betty is making a big mistake!"*

Laughter.

Next, Bob found Harold Neymeir reviewing drawings in his office. He repeated the "sales pitch," and Harold agreed as well.

Harold did comment, *"The old man is paying for everything? Marrying into a rich family—good planning!"*

Bob replied, *"Actually, the family is Middle America personified, but Betty's father has been saving for this her whole life. And you get to sponge off him—it's like winning the Publishers Clearing House prize without ever entering. Ralph Swenson is organizing the bachelor party, so he will be contacting you."*

Great! Now if Frank Baron agreed, the groomsmen were complete. Bob waited until after 10:00 a.m. to call Frank, assuming that a Massey retiree would be sleeping late. Frank answered the telephone on the second ring.

He said, *"Massey Chemical! Who the heck is calling me from Massey Chemical?"*

Bob replied, *"Frank, this is Bob Garver, I'm calling to tell you that your retirement is being cancelled. Just joking! How's retirement going?"*

Frank said, *"Great! I'm enjoying the time by working on honey-do projects. My wife has a list a mile long! What's going on?"*

Bob got to the point, *"Frank, I'm getting married on December 15, and I would really like it if you would be one of my groomsmen. I always thought you were a great boss, and super instrument engineer. Would you do it?"*

Frank said, *"With those compliments, how could I refuse? I'd be glad to. But who the heck would marry you?"*

Bob laughed and said, *"Her name is Betty Marcum, and she is a Deer Park police lieutenant. I figured that was the only way to keep me out of trouble! If I stray outside the lines, she will put me in jail!"*

Laughter on both ends.

"And remember that she's armed! So don't act up!"

Bob said, *"I know you live in Deer Park, but the father of the bride is paying for a hotel suite for each of the wedding party—you included. You can bring your wife—and she can bring her to-do list. Her father is picking up all the expenses, including dinner the night before the wedding. The bad news is that you will have to take off your Levi bib overalls and wear a tuxedo at the wedding! That may shock all the Massey folks in the wedding to see you that way. The entire olefins plant start-up team will be there, and Ralph Swenson from head office will be best man. You will be getting an official invitation that covers the time and place. I really appreciate this, Frank. And by the way, my compliments were real."*

It had been a great morning. The male side of the wedding party was organized and willing. Bob called Betty to let her know. She said that she would tell her mother and the wedding coordinator. She was in the process of contacting the women she wanted as her bridesmaids. Cindy Parker, her roommate, had already agreed to be her maid of honor. Betty asked if Bob was getting nervous since the wedding was getting close.

Bob told her, *"No. I'm leaning toward impatience—let's get it on!"*

Betty laughed, and said, *"Soon enough, big boy!"*

Bob said, *"Maybe I'll skip town!"*

Betty laughed and said, *"Remember, I have a friend in the FBI, you wouldn't stand a chance to avoid their dragnet!"*

Bob asked her for an update on the case. She indicated that they were close to having John Swisher dead to rights, but that they were trying to use him to find the Tin Man and pin down his involvement in the arson and attempted murders. Bob remarked that the recent weeks of "peace" were just fine with him, and he asked her to dinner at his apartment. Since he was no gourmet cook, he promised some great spaghetti complete with Ragù spaghetti sauce out of a jar. She said that would be just like being home.

CHAPTER 23

AN UPDATE AND DINNER

Following the phone call with Bob Garver, Betty decided to get an update from Mack Turner (alias Mack the Hack). He was located one floor down from her office, close to the main computer servers. Because of all the evidence against John Swisher, she had been able to get a rather loose warrant allowing the police to monitor Swisher's phones, both office and cell.

Betty asked Mack, *"So what has Swisher been up to?"*

Mack said, *"Mostly boring stuff, but you will remember your meeting with him where you almost gave him a heart attack. He followed that meeting with a big mistake. Since the warrant allowed us to listen in, we heard him call the Tin Man's burner phone. That gave us Tim Man's location, but unfortunately, we just missed catching him in Sugar Land. We did hear the Tin Man give him heck because he called his burner phone. He said he would destroy it and call him with another burner phone number. He also said that if Swisher called him again, he would personally come cram the phone down his throat. Since we were listening, when he called Swisher with the new number, we got it! That would normally let us track him, but he turned the phone off immediately following the call, and it has not been active since.*

"You will also remember Swisher offered the Tin Man an extra $5,000 to get Bob Garver killed right away—to be paid after his death. The Tin Man said he wanted the money up front and would call when he had set up a dead drop location. We've been listening for that call ever since."

Betty complimented Mack and told him to call her right away, day or night, if the dead drop call came in. She asked how he was handling the other shifts. Mack told her that they had it covered twenty-four hours a day, not to worry. Since police work involves many hours of waiting, Betty returned to her office and resumed her normal job.

That evening at six thirty, Betty drove over to Bob's apartment looking forward to his "gourmet" spaghetti dinner. He kissed her at the door and seated her in the living room area. He had a bottle of Blue Nun white wine chilled and open and poured them two glasses. Betty was pleasantly surprised, it was delicious.

She said, *"If this is what nuns drink, I may become a nun."*

Bob replied, *"Sorry, I have other plans for you that don't involve chastity."*

They both had a good laugh.

They moved to the dinner table at 7:00 p.m., and Bob brought in a tossed salad and garlic bread. He also refilled their wineglasses.

Betty said, *"I thought I was just going to get Ragù spaghetti! This is pretty fancy for someone who doesn't cook."*

Bob said, *"When I have a special guest, I go all out! Wait until you see dessert."*

They enjoyed their salad, bread, and wine—but they enjoyed their company most of all.

Bob and Betty walked into the kitchen area, and Bob tested the spaghetti by throwing a piece against the wall.

Betty said, *"What are you doing!"*

Bob replied, *"That is how great chefs test for al dente."*

Betty said, *"What's al dente?"*

Bob replied, *"For you uninitiated cooks, al dente describes pasta that is cooked just right. In Italian, it means 'to the tooth,' and one way to detect if spaghetti is al dente is to throw one piece against the wall. If it sticks, it is ready. And ours is ready."*

Betty laughed and said, *"That piece on the wall goes in your spaghetti, not mine!"*

While Bob mixed in the meatballs and poured the heated Ragù sauce over the spaghetti, she said, *"I expect you to cook every night after we are married!"*

Bob replied, *"Fat chance! And if you keep this up, you won't get any of this al dente spaghetti!"* They both laughed as Bob carried the meal back to the table. Betty commented that the spaghetti was the best she had ever eaten. Bob attributed that to the Ragù spaghetti sauce straight from the bottle. After some small talk about the weather and how the wedding plans were coming together, Betty told Bob about the conversation she had with Mack the Hack. She said she was in the waiting mode—waiting for the Tin Man to make the phone call about the dead drop.

For dessert, Bob had a surprise—carrot cake. He had found a recipe in an old *Betty Crocker Cookbook*. He told Betty that it was good, but wasn't as good as Treebeard's. That had become a standard line for them, and it never failed to get a smile. Betty fibbed and said it was better than Treebeard's. But they both knew it wasn't.

They washed the dishes together. Even work seemed like fun when they were together. Suddenly, they heard a cell phone ring back in the living area.

Betty said, *"That sounds like my ring. I've got to get it."*

Bob followed her into the living area while she answered her phone.

She said, *"Betty Marcum. Hi, Mack, what's happening?"* Pause. *"Okay, I'll be there in about twenty minutes. Make sure you record everything. See you."*

Bob asked, *"What's going on? A triple homicide?"*

Betty said, *"No—even better. Mack intercepted a call from the Tin Man's new burner phone to John Swisher. He was setting up a dead drop for the Tin Man to pay him an extra $5,000 for your murder."*

Bob said, *"What a great way to end our spaghetti supper! Do you want me to go with you? Or should I stay here and wait to be murdered?"*

Betty said, *"No, this is police work, I'll let you know how it turns out. And by the way, thanks for the wonderful dinner. Like I said, you can cook for us every night after we're married."*

They kissed at the apartment door, and Betty drove off into the night on the way to the Deer Park Police Department.

CHAPTER 24

THE TRAP AND CASING THE CHURCH

Since it was the evening shift, Betty arrived at the Deer Park Police Headquarters at the same time as Mack Turner (alias Mack the Hack). They walked down the main hallway to the server room where Sam Peck was on duty monitoring Swisher's calls. Sam worked directly for Mack and was an expert on phone tapping, cell phone location, and other clandestine computerese stuff. A small police department, like Deer Park, did not usually have someone like Sam. However, they had been very fortunate that Sam had interviewed for a police position, and after hiring him, they discovered this rich mine of talent. Mack asked Sam to tell Betty what he had told him on the phone.

Sam said that he had been getting bored looking for a call to the burner phone, which never came. And the phone taps on John Swisher's home and office phones provided no information related to the case. But a few hours ago, all that changed. The new burner phone, owned by the Tin Man, called John Swisher on his cell phone. That had allowed Sam to locate where the Tin Man was calling from; but better yet, they had direct surveillance on Swisher's cell phone, so they actually heard the discussion, and recorded it. Swisher was in a moving vehicle, headed northwest on Highway 290. A call for support from the Houston police did not produce results quick enough—the phone call ended before any action could be taken.

The recorded conversation was cryptic but informative.

The Tin Man started by saying, *"Swisher, you know who this is. Shut up and listen. I have planned the required action very soon, and you need to get me the extra funding."*

Swisher replied, *"How will you do it?"*

Tin Man's response was curt. *"Do you think I'm stupid! We can't discuss that on the phone, you butthead! I want you to take the extra funding we discussed to the waterwall in a manila envelope tomorrow at 11:30 p.m. Place it on the inside of the waterwall, close to the center column."*

Swisher said, *"Waterwall—what are you talking about? I don't have any idea where a wall of water is."*

The Tin Man responded, *"Look it up on the Internet—it is next to a very tall building near the Galleria—you will find it. That's it, I'm hanging up and will destroy this phone like I did the first burner phone. I will only talk with you one more time—after the planned action—and then, only if you have supplied the extra funds."* The Tin Man disconnected and smashed the burner phone.

Betty said, *"Wow! Do either of you know where this waterwall is?"*

Sam said, *"I'm pretty sure he was referring to the Hines Waterwall Park next to the Williams Tower in Houston's uptown district. The fountain and its surrounding park were built as an architectural attraction next to the tower."*

Mack added, *"That sounds right. It's not one of the biggest Houston attractions, but when I was a summer intern with Bechtel, it was visible from their offices. It gets confusing, because Williams Tower was once the Transco Tower, and the Waterwall was known as the Transco Waterwall and the Williams Waterwall prior to being renamed the Hines Waterwall Park. Actually, it is pretty impressive up close, and quite a few weddings are held there each year."*

Betty joked, *"Maybe we should move our wedding to the Waterwall!"*

Then she said, *"Fat chance. My mother would kill me if we moved things at this late date!"*

Betty added, *"Seriously, we need to get a plainclothes operation in place before tomorrow night. At that time of night, in an open park, it will be hard to remain undetected, but we have to wait for the money transfer to take place. In addition, Sam, can you get high-definition video surveillance set up before that time so we can record the dead drop and the pickup?"*

Using a German accent, Sam said, *"Your wish is my command, Commandant!"*

Mack said, *"Let's make sure the cameras are high-definition, and let's use two or three for reliability and view from differing angles. They need to adjust to the low light that will be available at that hour, none of that infrared stuff—which is always hard to read. These need to provide high-definition color videos and snapshots. Can you do that?"*

Sam said, *"I'll give it my best shot."*

Mack continued, *"They also need to be able to transmit the results at least a quarter mile to allow our van to park unseen. That's where we will be watching."*

Betty replied, *"I'll see if my friend at the Houston FBI Office will do me a favor. And I'll see if they have the equipment you need."*

Betty said, *"Okay, let's get going on this. Let me know if you need anything. I will call the Houston Police to let them know we are 'playing in their backyard,' and see if they want to participate. I suspect they will let us run the operation on our own and will try to stay out of the way. Sam, Mack, you guys have done a great job! If this goes well, we should be able to arrest the two perps. But the video will be critical as evidence! Keep me informed when you have the stakeout location and camera locations pinned down. I would like to see the system tested tonight, if possible, under actual light conditions. Okay—we don't have that much time—you guys get busy over at the Waterwall setting this up. And thanks again for your work."*

Betty called Jack Lentor at the FBI and said, *"Hey, Jack, remember you said to call you if I needed some more help?"*

Jack said, *"I remember—my big mouth has gotten me in trouble again, hasn't it?"*

Betty asked him about the remote low-light camera equipment that they would need to trap the arsonist. Jack said, *"We have just what you need, but for this one, I'll have to call in every favor I'm owed. Would you agree to one of our people helping to set this up?"*

Betty said, *"Sure. My guy is good, but this equipment is outside his normal expertise. I'm sure he would like working with your expert. And to add to the favor—I need the equipment set up and tested by tonight. We want to make sure it works at the same time a dead drop is to occur tomorrow night. We're lucky in one way—both nights are supposed to be clear with a third quarter moon. That should give us reasonable light."*

Jack said, *"Tonight!? You don't want much, do you? Okay, let me get busy on this. Where are the cameras to be set up?"*

Betty said, *"At the Hines Waterwall Park."*

Jack replied, *"Well, if we don't capture the culprits, at least we'll get some great photos of the waterwall."*

Betty passed this information on to Mark and Sam via cell phone since they were already on their way to the Waterwall. She said she would call them when she had more details. Sam remarked that he hoped the FBI equipment would pan out since he hadn't been sure he could get camera equipment that would meet the requirements.

While this discussion was going on, the Tin Man reversed his course on Highway 290 and headed for Deer Park. In case the burner phone was being traced, he had headed northeast to throw off any surveillance. But now his destination was the Faith Community Church in Deer Park. As he drove down the West Loop, one of the most heavily travelled highways in Texas, he dropped the burner phone out of his window and was pleased to see an 18-wheeler smash it to bits beneath its tires. At this time of day, it would take him about forty-five minutes to reach the church. His goal was to "case" the church for the "execution" during the wedding ceremony. He had scheduled a meeting with the pastor, lying about his intent to be married in the church. The pastor should be a rich source of information that he could use to plan the attack. He thought to himself, *The one witness to my arson has a short time to live.*

When he reached the church, before meeting with the pastor, he went into the main auditorium where the wedding would be held. He was pleased to see that there was a balcony across the entire width of the room. That would give him the high ground for setting up his shot. At the top of the balcony area, there was what appeared to be a sound booth with a window. Again, that was great; it would provide him with cover until the proper time. He climbed the stairs from the lobby to the balcony and concluded that it would make a quick exit path. If anyone tried to stop him, they would pay dearly.

The sound booth had a small room off the side where equipment was stored. There was space behind the equipment that would make an excellent hiding place prior to the hit. Next to the sound booth, there was another room that was equipped as a classroom. The two rooms were connected with a door, and the classroom offered another spot for cover.

The Tin Man's meeting with Pastor Don Lancy took a turn that he did not expect. He introduced himself as Michael Bernardino (a fake name) and said that he and his fiancée were looking for a church to get married in. He said that he had always admired this church for its beautiful building. The pastor asked him if he was a Christian. That was unexpected—but he said sure! The pastor then asked him to tell him how he was saved. Whoops! He shuffled a bit and said that he had always been a Christian. This was a red flag to Pastor Lancy. He explained that church policy prevented him from marrying any couples that were not Christians, and quoted scripture about not being unequally yoked.

He then explained the simple gospel to the Tin Man—that all have fallen short of the glory of God, that all are therefore sinners in the eyes of a holy God. He explained that there was absolutely nothing anyone could do to correct this by trying to please God, work as hard as they might. He told him that the penalty for being a sinner was death, eternity in hell. But the good news (the gospel) is that Christ took our sins and paid the penalty for them when He died on the cross. All we have to do is accept His completed work by faith, and we can have salvation—eternal life.

The pastor then asked if the Tin Man would like to accept Christ. Wow! This had not gone the way the Tin Man had intended. He hemmed and hawed, said he had another appointment, and rushed out of the office, into his car, and sped away. He had grown up in a family that infrequently went to church, but as soon as he was able, he stopped going at all. He never wanted to hear that "crap" again. But he admitted to himself that he had never heard the stuff that the pastor had explained to him. He was a hard man, so it was soon forgotten. Fortunately, his preliminary tour had provided him with the layout of the church auditorium, and now he could plan the upcoming attack.

CHAPTER 25

WEDDING PREPARATIONS

Betty was as busy as the proverbial "one-armed paper hanger," but gave her mother a call to see how the wedding plans were going. She told her that things were going very well, and gave the credit to Linda Marker, the wedding coordinator. She said she was just driving into Betty's apartment parking lot and would be staying in the extra room for a couple of days. She then said that seeing Betty was a must since she had a million things to consult her about. Betty immediately hopped in her car and drove to her apartment to see her mother.

The wedding announcements had been sent out, and her mother had already received several positive comments about the graphic design with the five-year-olds dressed in wedding clothes. But her mother questioned whether Betty was serious about inviting Jack Lentor, the FBI agent who had been Betty's beau a few years back. Betty said that Bob Garver was well aware of the former relationship and that he had been the one to suggest inviting him, since he had helped Betty out on the arson case.

Her mother said, *"You've got yourself a very special man there."*

Betty agreed, but noted that the fact Jack was now married didn't hurt.

Her mother said that they had reserved so many suites and rooms at the hotel, it was essentially theirs for the night. They had planned a roast beef dinner that night for those staying in the hotel. Because of the large amount of business, the hotel manager had bent over backward to please them and said that the dinner would be supplied at cost.

Betty's dad had been pleased at learning that fact and commented, *"Maybe that will keep us out of the poorhouse."*

Since the bridesmaids had all gone to school together, they chose not to bring their husbands (where they had one). So Marsha asked them if they would rather room together instead of having their own room. They thought that would be great and picked the roommate they were closest to.

Betty thought that was a great idea and commented, *"I'll bet Dad will like the idea of two less suites too!"*

Her mother again said that the money was not a problem. The groomsmen, on the other hand, were all bringing their wives, and so they were booked into individual hotel suites. Most of the men had already been fitted for their tuxedos, and the remaining guy would get it done tomorrow. Her mother had approved the red-and-green bow ties, and the supplier was throwing in red-and-green cummerbunds. She commented that it was going to look spectacular.

Betty told her mother that she had confirmed that the church organist and pianist were scheduled. Pastor Lancy had suggested a soprano, Mary Lenox, to sing prior to the service, since she had done this many times and received many compliments. Mary had a fine voice. Betty said that Mary would be combining romantic songs and Christian songs. Her mother confirmed Betty's father had already written the checks for the pastor and the musicians. He would now add the singer—he liked to stay ahead of the game.

Betty asked about the music for the reception. Her mother said that Linda Marker had suggested the group called the Easy Ensemble. They were presently playing nightly at a restaurant in Sugar Land. Marsha asked if Betty and Bob were available for dinner to take a look at them. Betty said, *"That's a good idea, but not for the next couple of nights, I have some police work I would be involved in."* She did not explain that she would be on stakeout trying to catch the Massey arsonist and his monetary sponsor, John Swisher. They scheduled it for the upcoming weekend, and Betty agreed to make sure Bob could make it.

Marsha had also confirmed that the church decorations coordinator had agreed to decorate both the wedding ceremony auditorium and the reception hall. She would be incorporating the fact that it was the

Christmas season and making sure Christ's birth was a main theme. To relieve her concerns about cost, Marsha had given her the check for $500. She seemed pleased with the amount.

This reminded Marsha to ask Betty when she could meet the wedding dress seamstress for a fitting. They agreed to work this into the upcoming weekend. Her mother assured her that the wedding dress was on schedule. The flowers for the wedding and reception had been ordered. Marsha asked if Betty was okay with lots of poinsettias as well as assorted Christmas cactus, holly, hypericum, amaryllis, ivy, and of course mistletoe. Betty remarked that her mother had talent in this area—maybe she should become a wedding consultant. Marsha thanked her, but said that Linda Marker, the actual wedding coordinator, and the flower supplier, had come up with the recommendations.

Marsha had asked Pastor Lancy to see if the church deacons could handle the setup and takedown of the tables and chairs in the reception hall. As it turned out, there was a Christmas celebration planned for the room during the previous week, so the wedding reception setup would not create any extra work for them. The pastor was pleased with Betty's father offering $1,000 to the building fund for the use of the hall. Marsha had also called Ralph Swenson to talk about how he planned to handle his master of ceremonies job. She commented that she was impressed with how much thought he had already put into the task. Ralph also described the bachelor's party that he had organized, but swore her to secrecy. He had already contacted all the men who would be attending. She told Betty that she thought Ralph Swenson would do a super job as best man.

They had originally selected Alaska salmon for the reception main course. The caterer was concerned about the difficulty in keeping the pre-prepared fish from drying out. He recommended a change to filet mignon steaks. The steaks could be prepared just before the reception dinner and sorted based on rare, medium rare, etc. so people could select the right steak for their particular taste while in the buffet line. Betty agreed with the change and said that she would advise Bob—although so far he had not seemed that interested in what they would be eating. He had said that he would have "other things" on his mind at that time.

Betty's mother said that they had contacted a travel agent to organize the honeymoon trip to Hawaii. So far, he was doing a good job. Their

United Airline and Aloha Airlines tickets were in hand. They were booked in the honeymoon suite at the Houston Airport Hotel for the night prior to the flight, and the limousine from the reception to the hotel had been reserved, as well as the limousine from the airport to their Deer Park apartment at the end of the trip. Since this was their first trip to Hawaii, the travel agent had reserved a four-wheel drive rental SUV on both islands. And a reservation had been made for their attendance at the obligatory luau.

On Kawaii, he had reserved the honeymoon suite with an ocean view at a hotel at Poipu Beach. He had marked up a map showing them how to get there from the Lihue Airport. The map also showed a possible route where they would see the Poipu Blowhole on a drive to Waimea Canyon to see the Kalalau Lookout. On another day, he had reserved space on a Wailua River Tour to the Fern Grotto. The drive to the river would take them past Opaekaa Falls, the Kilauea Lighthouse, Hanalei Bay, and end at Kee Beach, where they could climb a trail leading up to a place to view the rugged Na Pali Coast. On a third day, he had them scheduled for a helicopter tour of the island. This was the best way to see the Na Pali Coast, and the only way to see some of the beautiful waterfalls in the inner island.

After a flight on Aloha Airlines, to the Big Island of Hawaii, he had them staying in a condominium in Kailua. The four-wheel drive SUV would allow them to drive across the saddle between the volcanoes. Again, he had marked a route for them to see the Waipio Valley (the Valley of the Kings), Akaka Falls, Kahuna Falls, and Rainbow Falls. They were routed over the Chain of Craters Road, returning to the other side of the island by the drive across the saddle. On another day, he had them driving to Puuhonua o Honaunau (the Place of Refuge), a black sand beach, for a swim, and Ka Lae (the southernmost point in the United States). The travel agent realized that they were on a honeymoon, so he left plenty of leisure time for swimming or sunbathing. Betty said to her mother, *"I suspect that Bob has plans that don't involve being out in the sun!"* They laughed.

Betty showered her mother with compliments about how well she was coordinating everything. She asked her to make sure her father knew how much she appreciated that he was paying for it all. She commented that it was getting very close—and that she was beginning to get cold feet. Her mother explained that was a normal reaction for brides to have. She asked Betty if she really loved Bob.

Betty said, *"With all my heart, Mom!"*

Her mother said, *"Then don't worry about cold feet—he'll warm them up on the honeymoon!"*

"Oh, Mom!" Betty said.

And then she hustled back to the police department—there was too much to do, and so little time to do it!

CHAPTER 26

SETTING THE TRAP

Betty received a phone call from FBI agent Jack Lentor.

He said, *"I've called in every favor I have ever been owed! But we have the kind of expert you need for this. His name is Randy Simcon, and he tells me that with the clear skies tonight and tomorrow night, there should be no problem getting excellent high-definition color videos and photos."*

Betty responded, *"Jack, I'm sure glad I talked with you. The arsonist we're after has one death attributed to one of his Massey Chemical fires. We need to catch him. My two guys, Mack Turner and Sam Peck, are already at the Hines Waterwall. Any chance Randy Simcon can join them?"*

Jack said, *"Yep. In fact, my guy is standing here in my office. I know where the Waterwall is, so I will accompany him and do the introductions. Warn your guys we are coming."*

Betty asked, *"Will Randy have the camera equipment with him?"*

Jack said, *"Yes. We'll be coming in a van that is set up to install the equipment, so you should be ready to test it tonight."*

Betty said, *"Jack, you are* good!*"*

Jack replied, *"When you're right, you're right!"* ending the call with a laugh.

The Hines Waterwall Park was originally privately owned; however, it was now owned and operated by the City of Houston. Betty used another of her contacts in the Houston City Government to let them know about setting up temporary camera surveillance. They had no problem cooperating with the FBI on this.

Mack Turner and Sam Peck had reached the Hines Waterwall. They were in the process of driving around the park to determine the best locations for the cameras. They got Betty's call telling them that they were to coordinate with the FBI camera expert. This relieved Sam's mind about finding this type of high-definition equipment. The Waterwall is a multistory sculptural fountain shaped as a circle segment of about 120 degrees. The water is piped to the top of the structure, distributed along twelve distribution channels, and runs down the face of the fountain on both the inside and outside of the circle segment. It is quite beautiful.

Since the Tin Man's instructions were to leave the envelope on the inside, against the center column, one of the best places for a camera was on top of the fountain, shooting downward from the side. They hoped the FBI expert had a way to get to the top and that his camera equipment was battery powered. The front of the circle segment was occupied by a brick building façade containing three arches. This gave a "framed view" of the Waterwall and was used as a backdrop for weddings. Two more spots for cameras were on the top of this façade, on each end, facing down toward the center column.

*   *   *

About this time, Jack Lentor and his FBI camera expert, Randy Simcon, arrived in the unmarked FBI panel truck. Jack introduced himself and Randy to Mack Turner and Sam Peck.

Mack said, *"Betty gave us a heads-up that you were coming."*

Sam added, *"I'm sure glad we are using your equipment. I wasn't sure I could locate high-definition cameras that would give good videos and photos in low-light conditions. I understand that you have the right equipment."*

Randy Simcon said, *"I think you will be impressed with the photographic equipment we have brought. How many cameras do you think we will need?"*

Mark showed them the three locations they thought would capture the dead drop, and Randy suggested that they add three more cameras shooting from ground level—two into the sides of the circle segments, and one shooting directly into the center building façade arch. He explained that they had a clever ground mount that looks exactly like a floodlight; in fact, it included a floodlight that would help produce that illusion. An added benefit, the floodlight would also add to the light on the subject.

Sam asked Randy how he could get to the tops of the fountain and the building façade. On the roof of the van, he showed him an extension ladder that was the longest extension ladder he had ever seen.

"No problem," Randy said.

Jack Lentor said, *"If anyone asks you what you are doing, tell them you are setting up cameras for a TV commercial. If they pursue it, have them check with John Lever, at the City of Houston—he knows what we are doing and will squelch any nosy people."*

Sam asked Randy how the cameras were powered and how far they would transmit.

Randy said, *"Each camera has a battery and backup battery, each of which will power the camera and transmitter for one month. The floodlight camera batteries are only good for forty-eight hours. The signal transmission is good for up to a mile. One of the things we will need to do is locate a good spot for our van to monitor the cameras."*

While Randy and Sam got busy setting up the six cameras, Mack took Jack Lentor to a parking spot for the van next to Williams Tower. The van would not be visible from the Waterwall.

The camera installation took about three hours, and all but Randy Simon got in the van to test it out. The six cameras bracketed the dead drop location from the top upper sides, ground level sides, and center. For the test, Randy played the part of John Swisher and dropped an envelope by the center column. He approached the drop point from both sides and through the building façade. In each case, he was easy to identify, and they got both videos and still photos that were outstanding in clarity. Randy walked over to the van, and using the cameras' remote controls, he fine-tuned the direction the cameras were pointed. Everyone agreed they were ready to test the system that night under moonlit conditions. Dusk was beginning to fall. They all went out for dinner at the close-by Chipotle Mexican Grill, on the FBI's tab.

Betty was not going to be left out of this dead drop camera test. Jack Lentor had called her when the setup was close to finished. She had expected the call and was on her way to the Waterwall. She joined the crew at Chipotle—why not, it was on the FBI's tab! She congratulated the team and said that they had accomplished a miracle in the short time they had.

Jack said, *"Well, after all, this is the FBI, we major in miracles!"*
Everyone laughed.

Betty said, *"As long as you pay for dinner, we'll laugh at all your jokes!"*
Again laughter.

Jack said, *"But honestly, after we identified the Tin Man via facial identification, we found out that this guy is wanted by the FBI too. My management gave the okay to help you in any way we can."*

The food was excellent, the conversation lively, and time passed quickly.

The dead drop was to take place at 11:30 p.m. the next day. So the team loaded up in the van, with Betty following in her car. Randy Simon, the FBI's camera guru, agreed to once again play the part of John Swisher and the Tin Man. They would run a test for Betty's benefit at 10:30 p.m. to confirm everything was working and show her their handiwork. Then, again at 11:30 p.m., so they would repeat the test under the exact moonlight conditions they expected tomorrow. They parked the van in the spot by Williams Tower, and Betty lent her car to Randy to get to the Waterwall.

The van was fairly crowded with four people in it. Randy had brought Sam Peck up to speed on operating the van readout equipment. For half an hour they entertained themselves by watching the waterwall from the various angles. It truly was a beautiful attraction. But then, at 10:30 p.m., a person in a hooded jacket came into view. It was Randy, again playing the part of John Swisher. He came in from the left-hand side, and Sam used the right-hand ground camera to zoom in on him. The high-definition camera made it quite clear that this was Randy Simon. He went to the center column and put the envelope down. As he left via the building façade, the center arch ground camera was zoomed in on his face. No doubt—it was Randy. They then ran the test over with Randy entering and leaving different ways. They reviewed the videos and photos, then called Randy to let him know the test was over.

At 11:30 p.m., the "moonlight test" was started. It was amazing how well the cameras captured the scene in this low-light condition. This time, Randy came in from the front building façade. The two upper-façade roof cameras picked up his side view clearly as he came into the open area, and he made the "mistake" of looking up at the moon. The two Waterwall cameras showed Randy's upturned face from both sides, and Sam was able to zoom in and get a great picture. Randy dropped off the envelope and headed out the left side. The left-side camera got the best picture of all since he essentially walked within ten feet of it.

Betty called Randy and announced to him and the crew, *"We're ready. You guys have done a remarkable job. Jack, I couldn't have done this without you—I'll call you tomorrow morning, and we can discuss how to monitor and catch these guys. I owe you big-time! Okay, folks, let's meet back here at 10:30 p.m. tomorrow, and we'll catch ourselves an arsonist and a murderer."*

CHAPTER 27

THE MOUSE GOES FOR THE CHEESE

When Betty got home, although it was late, she called Bob to update him on the Waterwall Park trap. He said that he wanted to be part of the team to catch the Tin Man, but Betty put the kibosh on that. She told him that this was police work and that the bad guys carried guns. Bob thanked her for waking him to tell him the good news, but in the back of his mind, he decided to find a way to take part in the capture.

First thing when Betty got to work in the morning, she called Jack Lentor to discuss the tactics of the capture. He had some good news. He had brought his boss at the FBI up to date on their progress in finding and capturing the arsonist Marcus Stalinbeck, who was also wanted by the FBI. He was pleased and reiterated that Jack could have access to any of the FBI's resources.

Jack sent Betty a map of the Waterwall area as well as an aerial photo covering the same ground. They decided that the surveillance van would park where it parked on the previous night. It would be manned by Mack (the Hack) Turner, Deer Park Police; and Randy Simcon, FBI, since they were now both experts on the camera technology and its operation.

Since John Swisher would be dropping off the money first, they didn't want to pick him up until the Tin Man had collected the money, in case he was watching the dead drop area. So they positioned the remaining Deer Park police, Betty Marcum and Joe Lighten, in a car at the southeast corner of the park at the corner of Hidalgo Street and Post Oak Boulevard since Post Oak provided quick access to the easiest escape route by paralleling the West Loop going south and entering the Southwest Freeway. As a precaution, Betty called her contact at the Sugar Land Police to ask them to be on alert in case this escape route was used. He assured her that the officers on shift that night would be updated on the escape route possibility, and be ready to assist.

The team of FBI agents would be scattered and hidden throughout the park. There would be others in unmarked cars by the Williams Tower, along Waterwall Road, Hidalgo Street, and Post Oak Boulevard. In theory, this should make the arrest of John Swisher easy or, in the worst case, allow them to chase down any car he used for escape. This surveillance would also allow them to detect when the two culprits entered the park. All police and agents would be equipped with radios, and overall coordination would be by the surveillance team in the FBI van. Since it was a relatively large team, they agreed they would arrive at 10:00 p.m. to scout out positions and get ready for John Swisher at 11:30 p.m. Well-thought-out plans. But as they say, *"The best-laid plans of mice and men often go astray."*

At 10:00 p.m., after dark, the team converged on Waterwall Park, and the FBI agents fanned out to find good hiding places. This was not too difficult, since there were numerous shrubs and trees throughout the park. The surveillance team in the van was busy checking out the cameras and adjusting their positions to pick up anyone entering the inner area of the Waterwall. All the equipment was working perfectly. Jack Lentor circulated through the park to make sure his agents were well hidden and knew what to expect—he then joined the surveillance team in the FBI trailer. Radio contact was made with all parties, including the various cars protecting the escape routes. They were ready.

At 11:15 p.m., a car on Hidalgo Street radioed that a car was pulling in to the park and stopping. Hidalgo was on the backside of the Waterwall, but was its closest street. The occupant sat in the car until 11:30 p.m. Then he got out and started walking toward the Waterwall. He appeared to be carrying something under his arm, which could be the envelope containing the money. He went in the west side of the Waterwall, and the surveillance team captured it on video and got a few good photos. It was John Swisher without question. This information was radioed to the rest of the team.

The overhead cameras followed Swisher as he looked for the dead drop spot. He seemed to be having trouble deciding which column was the proper drop spot. He looked around, as if trying to spot the pickup person; and in fact, he gave indication that he might have seen someone lurking in the shadows. The surveillance cameras captured all of this on video, and they took several more photos, from overhead, and from the left- and right-side cameras.

Mack the Hack said, *"We've got this guy dead to rights! These videos and photos will convince any jury."*

Lentor commented, *"Let's make several eight-by-ten-inch glossies for his scrapbook!"* (Laughter.)

Swisher finally decided on the column for the dead drop and placed the envelope containing the $5,000 at its base. He made one last look around, focusing on the shrubs where apparently he thought he might have seen something or someone. He decided that it was his imagination, and he started walking back to his car. Via radio, everyone was reminded not to arrest him yet and advised to be on the alert for the Tin Man to enter the park and pick up the money. The original plan was to arrest Swisher as soon as the money was picked up, followed by the arrest of the Tin Man. But Swisher reached his car, started it, and headed down Hidalgo Street to Post Oak Boulevard before the Tin Man appeared.

Two cars immediately began to follow him. Lt. Betty Marcum was in the first, and an FBI agent was in the second. As expected, on Post Oak Boulevard, Swisher paralleled the West Loop until Post Oak entered the Southwest Freeway. At that point, he sped up and crossed over into the far-left fast lane. The two chase cars turned on their lights and sirens. A high-speed chase ensued, reaching speeds of 120 mph. Betty radioed ahead to her prearranged contact on the Sugar Land police, and fifteen minutes later, as the cars approached their area, the Sugar Land police had set up their cars in a roadblock to force Swisher to stay in the left-hand lane.

Cars ahead of Swisher were waved on through. He sighted the roadblock and tried to speed through, but the police threw down spike strips. Swisher ran over the spike strips, and all four tires blew out. He lost control, the car bounced off the center concrete barrier, flipped on its side, and slid across four lanes to a screeching halt on the side of the freeway. Somehow he managed to escape any serious injuries, only suffering a bloody nose when the airbag inflated.

Within minutes, Swisher was extracted from the car, handcuffed, and placed in the back of the FBI's car. Then they quickly cleared the freeway since traffic was backing up on the heavily travelled road even after midnight. Since the car had slid off the side, it would wait until a tow truck could be arranged by the Sugar Land Police. One of the mice had taken the cheese, and the trap had closed.

Betty thanked the Sugar Land police profusely and said, *"If you guys ever need anything from the Deer Park Police, you let me know. You did a great job!"*

However, "back at the ranch," as they say in the old cowboy movies, no one had picked up the dead-dropped envelope. Everyone was on high alert, but it was almost 12:30 p.m. What had happened to the Tin Man? Had he detected their trap? Jack Lentor warned his team via radio to stay put and stay alert. Suddenly, a buzzing noise was heard coming from the north. It got louder, and the FBI cars by Williams Tower radioed that, whatever it was, it was coming closer. They said that the noise seemed to be coming south on Post Oak Boulevard. It soon became apparent that the roar was coming from a motorcycle. When it passed the car parked at Williams Tower, it continued for about two hundred yards, then jumped the curb, entering Hines Waterwall Park, and headed for the Waterwall. One of the FBI agents who knew cycles radioed that the motorcycle was a Honda Rebel 500 cycle and commented that they ran about $6,000, noting that it would be very hard to follow with cars.

As soon as the motorcycle entered the park, it accelerated across the grass, throwing grass and dirt every which way. It headed directly for the east entrance of the Waterwall, climbed a few steps, and entered the inner circle area of the Waterwall. The rider accelerated over to the center, slammed on his brakes, skidding to a stop by the center column where the envelope had been placed. He picked up the envelope, stuffed it into his leather jacket, and accelerated toward the west side of the Waterwall.

Suddenly, out of the bushes on his left, a figure jumped out grabbing the rider, knocking him off and putting the cycle on its side. The unknown figure was knocked out momentarily. The rider quickly got up, ran to the cycle and righted it, and zoomed west across the grass onto Waterwall Drive. With a squeal of tires, he turned north on Waterwall Drive. Accelerating, he sped by Williams Tower, turning west on Alabama Street. The FBI car on Waterwall Drive was facing the wrong way. It took several seconds for them to react, get the car turned around, and begin to chase the motorcycle. It was a lost cause, given the maneuverability of the cycle, which began making multiple turns, including going through alleys and across unoccupied fields. Within ten minutes, the FBI car radioed back to the team that the Tin Man had escaped. Jack Lentor put out an APB, but the likelihood of making an arrest was fading quickly.

The surveillance cameras had taken excellent videos and photos of the dead drop pickup. However, the Tin Man was wearing his motorcycle helmet, with the face shield closed, and they were essentially useless unless you were trying to make a Honda motorcycle commercial. However, the cameras did reveal something. They revealed who knocked the cyclist off his bike—it was Bob Garver! This information was radioed to the team, and the closest agent got to Bob in time to see him pick himself up off the ground where the Tin Man had knocked him cold. Surprisingly, he was not hurt, other than his pride.

The FBI agent used some language unfit for church and then said, *"What the heck did you think you were doing? Jumping on a moving motorcycle? You're nuts!"*

Bob agreed, *"Yep, that's me—nuts."*

The agent asked, *"Where did you come from?"*

Bob said, *"I've been at the park since this morning. I've been hiding out since then, waiting for the dead drop to occur. I was beginning to think it would never happen."*

The FBI guy repeated himself, *"You're nuts!"*

Jack radioed the bad news about losing the Tin Man to Betty in Sugar Land.

She said, *"Jack, don't worry, we'll get him. At least we caught one of the mice—Swisher is in handcuffs."*

Jack replied, *"And we have enough evidence on him to send him up the river for a long time. We can show the jury eighty-by-ten glossy photos of him at the dead drop, as well as entertaining videos."*

Then Jack told Betty the shocker—that Bob Garver had attempted to jump the motorcyclist from hiding and had knocked him off the cycle temporarily.

She said, *"WHAT! You've got to be kidding! Wait until I get a hold of him! I made it clear that he was not to be here, that this was police work. Is he okay?"*

Jack said, *"Yes—he's okay—a little shaken from getting knocked out by the impact. But now he's as feisty as ever, and claiming that he almost caught the Tin Man. I have to admit, he came closer to it than we did."*

Betty said, *"I'm headed back to Deer Park to put Swisher behind bars, but you tell Bob that I'm gunning for him."*

Jack laughed, thankful that he was not in Bob Garver's shoes.

CHAPTER 28

INTERROGATION

When Bob came down from his apartment the next morning, there was a police car waiting for him. The Deer Park policeman would not take no for an answer—he was taken to the police department and personally delivered to Betty Marcum's office. Betty had fire in her eyes!

She said, *"What did you think you were doing! You could have been killed! I ought to shoot you myself!"*

Bob shrugged, and said, *"It seemed like a good thing to do at the time. And I almost caught him! Actually, I was pretty lucky. He didn't realize I was the witness that was his target. He could have shot me and ended it right there!"*

Betty yelled, *"You almost caught him? You almost got yourself killed! And you did get yourself beaten to a pulp by that motorcycle! I don't want to marry someone beaten to a pulp!"*

Bob looked at Betty and said, *"Yeah, but remember this—this beaten pulp still loves you."*

The fire went out of Betty's eyes, and she softened and said, *"Bob— for a minute, I thought I had lost you. Don't ever do that to me again."*

Bob said, *"Never! I'm through with police work."*

Betty said, *"The reason I had you brought in was to see if you saw anything that might be of value."*

Bob thought for a minute and said, *"Well, I was only knocked out for a second or two. But I saw that he was completely covered by his leather outfit and his helmet. After I knocked him off his cycle, he quickly got up, ran over to the cycle, set it up, and took off. But I did notice that he limped, just like the man I saw at the chemical plant. This was definitely the Tin Man."*

Betty said, *"We were already convinced about that, but your eyewitness viewpoint, now and from the chemical plant, confirms it."*

*   *   *

John Swisher had been arrested, read his Miranda rights, and was waiting for his lawyer to show up. Betty arranged to have him placed in an interrogation room. Armed with the videos and photos, Betty thought this was going to be fun watching him squirm. She invited Bob to watch from the adjoining room that was separated by a one-way mirror. Apparently, she was cooling off. Swisher's lawyer was "Bull Dog" Sumner, who was famous for defending folks on the seedier side of the law. He advised his client not to say a word. He asked Betty what Swisher was being charged with. Betty said that multiple charges were still being developed, but as a minimum, it would be conspiracy to commit arson, resisting arrest, and conspiracy to commit murder. In addition, she said that the Security and Exchange Commission (SEC) would be pursuing insider trading charges in civil court; however, since the insider trading ties in with the arson charge, it would also be used in the criminal court case.

Sumner said, *"You better have lots of evidence to prove all that."*

Betty said, *"You bet! I've been in this business a lot of years, but I've never seen anyone accumulate so much evidence against themselves."*

Sumner said, *"Okay, let's see it."*

Betty began by describing the "coincidences" between Swisher's short sales of stock happening just before the multiple fires and explosion at the Massey plant. She pointed out the fact that due to the huge drop in stock value, he had made over $500,000, which he deposited in an offshore account in the Cayman Islands.

Sumner said, *"Short sales are not illegal. Offshore accounts are not illegal. You can't prove that my client had prior knowledge of the Massey fires."*

Betty smiled and said, *"Correct, but just wait—there's more to be considered."*

She went on to describe the arsonist that was involved in the fires and explosion and that Swisher had made and received multiple phone calls from him on his burner phone.

"That's no proof. There's nothing illegal about talking with someone, even if it is on a disposable phone."

Betty said, *"But isn't it interesting how the one who benefited from the short sale made several calls to the arsonist who caused the fires that made the short sale pay off like a slot machine? By the way, there is a witness who can identify the arsonist, and there have been at least five attempts on his life. These attempts have been linked to that same arsonist, and it is interesting that your client transferred $50,000 from his offshore account to the arsonist just prior to one of the attempts to kill the witness. It has become obvious that the arsonist was paid that $50,000 to hire someone to kill the witness. Fortunately, the hired killer ended up getting shot herself, and $25,000 was found in her possession. What a coincidence!"*

The lawyer asked who the witness was. Betty said that would be revealed later, prior to the trial—since his life was obviously in danger.

Then Betty dropped the bomb. *"As I said, the original payment was for the murder of the witness. But the arsonist had botched the job so many times that your client made the mistake of talking to him on another burner phone, thinking that we could not trace the call. They were wrong—we had a warrant and have that call recorded. You can listen to it later, but Swisher essentially offers an additional $5,000 if the arsonist will make sure the witness gets killed quickly. They set up a dead drop location for the transfer of the money."*

The lawyer gave Swisher a quick look. He said, *"How do you know he was not paying the man for a new lawn mower?"*

Betty had to laugh.

She said, *"Yeah, I usually pay $5,000 for my lawn mowers by dropping off the money in the middle of the night at the Hines Waterwall, don't you? The clincher is that we have your client on both video and in high-resolution photos actually placing the money at the drop site. In addition, we have videos and photos of the arsonist picking up the money. I'll be glad to show them to you after this meeting. Then, your client left the drop site and fled in a high-speed chase down the Southwest Freeway, wrecking his car prior to capture by the police. I don't think the jury will have much trouble putting all of this information together for a conviction. These are not the behaviors of an innocent man."*

The lawyer said, *"I want to meet this arsonist. Where is he?"*

Betty was forced to acknowledge that he was not yet in custody, but said that would soon be corrected.

The lawyer said, *"A lot of this so-called evidence is circumstantial. I'll have my client out tomorrow, and it is obvious that bail will not be a problem."*

That was not good news to Bob, who was still watching from the adjoining room. Swisher was returned to his cell, awaiting the hearing before the judge.

Bob and Betty met in her office.

Bob complimented her on her interrogation technique, but she said, *"Unfortunately, the lawyer is right that much of the evidence is circumstantial. But I have seen people convicted on much less evidence than this."*

Bob said, *"The key piece that is missing is the Tin Man. Have they found him?"*

Betty said, *"No. They found his motorcycle out in Katy, Texas, but he was nowhere around, and there were no witnesses that saw him leave it there. But remember, Bob, from the Tin Man's perspective, you are the biggest piece missing. You are the key witness that can place him at the fires, at the apartment attack, and at the dead drop payment. You need to be ultracareful! I don't want to lose you before I marry you."*

She joked, *"After that, it's okay!"* (Laughter).

At that point, Betty said that she had to run. Bob asked why.

She said, *"Your memory is going—tonight is the bridal shower at the church. And don't forget that you have to make an appearance at 9:00 p.m."*

Bob said, *"Oh my gosh, I had forgotten, I'm sorry. Why do I have to come?"*

Betty said, *"It is tradition for the groom to make an appearance."*

Bob said, *"I'll be there, but it sounds like I'm a slab of meat being shown to the lions."*

Betty replied, *"You do remember that the wedding is this Saturday!?"*

Bob said, *"You bet! I may even show up for it."*

They laughed, and updated each other regarding how the wedding plans were proceeding. It was all coming together!

At 9:00 p.m., Bob showed up at the bridal shower. Surrounded by about fifty women, he did indeed feel like a slab of beef. Betty tried to make him feel comfortable by introducing him to her friends, and he guessed that it was worth the embarrassment since Betty got a "pile" of presents.

As he was getting into his car to leave, he said to Betty, *"My bachelor party is tomorrow night. You will need to make an appearance—it is tradition."*

She replied, *"No, it's not!"*

Bob said, *"Turnabout is fair play! We'll time it so that you arrive just in time to see the naked lady pop out of the cake!"* (Laughter). *"No—you can't come to my bachelor party—you might see the dark side of me and decide to marry someone else."*

Betty said, *"No way, Jose, you're not getting out of this that easily!"*

They kissed passionately, Betty went back to the shower, and Bob headed to his apartment.

CHAPTER 29

THE BACHELOR PARTY

When Bob arrived back in his apartment, the message light was blinking on his machine. The message was from his best man, Ralph Swenson, reminding him that his bachelor party was tomorrow, Friday, at 7:30 p.m. at the Deer Park Hotel, where the wedding party was staying. Ralph had reserved the hotel's conference room for the event. Knowing Ralph, this worried Bob a bit, since Ralph had been known to go to extremes in the past. Bob called him and left a message that he would be there with bells on, reminding him that the men in the wedding party should check into their rooms ahead of time. That would allow them to "crash" following the party, just in case.

Bob had taken three weeks of vacation, knowing that he would be busy prior to the wedding and recognizing, of course, that they would be in Hawaii for two weeks on their honeymoon. He made a quick call to Betty's mother, who assured him that everything was ready, all he had to do was show up. He thanked her for all her work—she appreciated that, and it reinforced her belief that Betty was getting a good man.

True to his word, Bob checked into the hotel around 6:00 p.m. on Friday and showed up at the bachelor party at exactly 7:30 p.m. Ralph Swenson greeted him at the door and handed him a big green cigar. Bob questioned whether the hotel allowed smoking.

Ralph said, *"I had a talk with the manager—he responded favorably to my 'green, rectangular' arguments!"*

Quite a few men were already there, and Bob noted that they were all smoking the big green cigars—it began to resemble the California air quality during fire season. So he lit up. The men from the wedding party were there, of course—and there were many others from both Massey head office and the Massey olefins plant, as well as from the church. Bob and Ralph walked around the room shaking hands with all of the attendees, and Bob took some good-natured ribbing about the upcoming nuptials. Never one to ignore a challenge, he held his own.

Since it was late, most of the men had eaten dinner; but Ralph had a buffet spread out on a series of tables. There were hundreds of shrimp, mini-tacos, meatballs, sausages, and lots of other diet-busting treats.

Bob told Ralph, *"This is great, Ralph, but I may need to call and get a larger tuxedo!"*

Ralph said, *"I had to spend your future father-in-law's money somehow! Just make believe it is Christmas already. Everybody overeats on Christmas!"*

That was enough of an excuse for Bob, and he loaded up his plate.

Ralph had also arranged for an open bar, and most of the men were already taking advantage of it. Bob was a "big drinker"—he might have one glass of wine once a year. This being a reasonably important occasion, he asked the bartender for a glass of white wine. He took some ribbing for it, being called a "teetotaler."

He replied, *"No, I'm a* white-wine-totaler."

Then he shot back, *"Somebody needs to stay sober to make sure you drunks can find your rooms! Plus—I don't want you to have to carry me down the aisle tomorrow!"* (Laughter.)

After everyone was there, Ralph told Bob he was now going to embarrass him.

Bob said, *"I don't embarrass easily."*

Ralph brought in an inflatable woman and told Bob he had to introduce her to three men as his intended bride. Bob played along, and it went over pretty well, getting plenty of laughs. Then Ralph asked for two volunteers to try convincing Bob that he was making a big mistake. At the end of that, Ralph brought out a ball and chain and hung it around Bob's neck. It got a little raunchy when Ralph told Bob that he needed some instructions for his wedding night and that he was the man to give them. Although not in great taste, fortunately Ralph didn't get too carried away.

He then had Bob put on a T-shirt that said, *"It's all over now!"*

Ralph ended the teasing by challenging the way a bride throws her bouquet backward to see who will be the next bride.

He said, *"The groom, and his wedding party, shouldn't be left out of that tradition."*

He then gave Bob a pair of women's panties and asked him to throw them back over his shoulder to the crowd of men behind him. It was amazing how many men fought to make the catch. Jack Lentor, the FBI agent, was the "winner."

He said, *"I'm not sure my wife will let me marry someone else!"* (Laughter.)

Betty had made sure Jack was invited to the wedding and bachelor party. Even though he had once dated Betty, Bob had begun to really like the guy—and of course, it didn't hurt at all that his people had saved his life at the Waterwall. It also didn't hurt that he was already married. Obviously, he was familiar with the arson/murder case, and he might come in handy if anything unusual happened during the wedding or reception.

It was a great party, and Bob thanked Ralph Swenson for all the effort he had put into it.

Ralph said, *"No problem—especially since your new father-in-law paid for it."*

Bob said, *"And I especially thank you that there wasn't a stripper jumping out of a cake!"*

Ralph said, *"What makes you think there isn't one? The party's not over yet!"* Pause. *"No—per your request, we tried to keep the party civil, and prevent the police from dragging you off, since your new wife is a cop. It would be bad form for her to have to bail you out for the wedding!"*

At 11:00 p.m., Bob excused himself by saying, *"I have something important to do tomorrow—I'm not sure what it is, but I better get some sleep."*

Everybody came by and shook his hand. It had been a super party—which continued on in his absence until around 1:00 a.m.

The next morning, there were a few men who had hangovers, but Betty's mother and the wedding coordinator started "herding the cats." As the song from the Music Man says, she would "get them to the church on time." The wedding was scheduled to start at 1:00 p.m.

CHAPTER 30

THE WEDDING

Following the messed-up dead drop, the Tin Man had used the maneuverability of his motorcycle to evade the FBI. He then raced out to Katy, Texas, where he had a plain gray sedan waiting. No one saw him make the switch. Using this car, he drove northeast to Livingston, Texas, and rented a hotel room, paying for a week in advance.

It was now the night prior to the wedding. He headed southwest on the Eastex Freeway toward Houston, went east on Beltway 8, crossed over the ship channel bridge, and arrived at the Deer Park Faith Community Church around midnight. He parked several blocks away and walked to the church. Entering the premises was no problem for him. They had a few surveillance cameras, but when he visited the church previously, he had located them all, and they were easily avoided. Years ago, he had taken an excellent locksmith course on the Internet and was proficient in picking locks, using the tools the course had supplied. After letting himself in through a door that did not have an alarm, he locked the entry behind him; and in a few minutes, he had entered the main auditorium where the wedding was to be held. He confirmed there was no one around.

Returning to the lobby, and using the small LED light on his cell phone, he climbed the stairs from the lobby to the balcony. After again checking to make sure he was alone, he opened the door to the sound booth and unpacked his .30-06 Springfield rifle. The ledge on the sound booth window would be ideal to steady the rifle for the kill shot.

When he was last in the church, he had estimated the distance from the sound booth to the altar. Visiting his local gun range, he had set a target at that distance and adjusted the riflescope. He was satisfied after he was able to place ten consecutive rounds in the center ring. Now he thought, *All I need is my live target!* He had brought a sleeping bag, so he hunkered down for the night, setting his wristwatch to vibrate and awaken him at 6:30 a.m.

*   *   *

The wedding coordinator had organized a quick buffet lunch in the hotel conference room for the men and their wives at eleven thirty, since it would be a while until the meal at the reception. The bride and bridesmaids had lunch in the hotel restaurant. Being in the same hotel, Betty's mother was concerned that Betty and Bob would see each other before the wedding—absolutely forbidden for some unknown reason! At twelve noon, the two limousines arrived—one for the men, one for the women. They parked at separate hotel exits so Betty and Bob would not see each other.

The women's limo left ten minutes before the men. When they arrived at the church, they were met by Don Lancy, the pastor, and taken to the bridal waiting room off the lobby behind the auditorium. The men arrived a few minutes later and accompanied the pastor to a room just off the auditorium stage, awaiting the beginning of the service. The pastor said that his deacons were placing attendees in the left or right section depending on whether they were friends of the bride or groom. He said that the auditorium was filling up fast.

Bob asked Ralph Swenson if he had the ring.

Ralph faked surprise and said, *"I thought you had it!"*

But he finally said, *"Yes, I have it."*

Whew!

Bob said, *"Ralph, I'm nervous enough already! Don't kid about things like that!"*

*   *   *

The Tin Man had been awakened by his watch at 6:30 a.m. There were two rooms off the sound room. One was a small storeroom where various video and sound equipment were stored. The other was a slightly larger room used for a Sunday school class. The Sunday schoolroom was accessible from either the sound room or the main auditorium balcony. Tin Man rolled up his sleeping bag and moved all of his gear to the storeroom, finding a spot behind some storage shelves where, if the soundman came in, he couldn't be seen. Then he checked the sound room again to make sure he had removed all evidence of his presence. He would stay hidden in the storeroom until the church soundman had adjusted the sound system during the prewedding music. Then, as he adjusted the pastor's microphone for the wedding vows, he would strike, knocking him cold with a stun gun.

He had been in this business for quite a few years and used to just knock someone out by whacking their head. But technology had moved on, and today, the best method of knocking someone out was definitely a stun gun. Also called an electroshock weapon, a stun gun uses a temporary high-voltage, low-current electrical discharge to override the body's muscle-triggering mechanisms. They are relatives of cattle prods, which have been around for over one hundred years. The victim is immobilized via two metal probes connected via wires to the stun gun. When shot, the recipient feels pain and is momentarily paralyzed. The Tin Man had researched stun guns and found one that was relatively noiseless.

He thought, *The new technology is making my job easier—and fun!*

He was ready—now the wait began.

* * *

Bob Garver, Ralph Swenson, and the rest of the groomsmen were with Pastor Lancy in the room off the auditorium. As is typical, Bob was nervous, and the other men were both encouraging him and kidding him about it. Fifteen minutes before the ceremony, the church pianist began playing, and the crowd, which was still filing in, quieted down. The music was outstanding, and then the church organist joined in on the songs, and the combination was like hearing music piped in directly from heaven. The church soprano sang like an angel.

At five minutes before the ceremony, Pastor Lancy walked out on the stage. The music stopped, and he welcomed the visitors to the church. He then signaled for Bob Garver and the men to come out on the stage, which they did.

* * *

In the sound booth, the soundman adjusted the pastor's microphone volume and leaned back to relax. The Tin Man, in his gum-soled shoes, noiselessly sneaked out of the storeroom, walked quickly across the sound room, and fired his stun gun. There was very little noise, and that was covered by the pastor making his announcements. The stun gun metal probes pierced the skin on the soundman's back, making him jerk as though every muscle in his body contracted at once—and the man crumpled down, eased to the floor by the Tin Man. He dragged him out of the way and used duct tape to tape his mouth and tape his hands behind his back.

He quickly got his rifle from the storeroom and got seated at the sound room window, ready to fire. To give everything a last check, he quickly used the riflescope to sight in on Bob Garver's chest, then sat back to wait for the ideal moment. He planned to fire just at the moment when Garver was supposed to say, *"I do."* That seemed appropriate for all the trouble he had put him through.

* * *

Jack Lentor, the FBI agent, was seated up front on the outside aisle of the bride's side of the church. The auditorium seating curved around so that everyone had a good view of the stage where Sunday sermons and musical activities took place. Jack was looking around the auditorium at exactly the moment that Tin Man did his final check of the riflescope. When he saw the rifle barrel come out of the sound room, he reacted immediately. Sizing up the auditorium, he quickly determined that the sound room was only accessible from the balcony. He headed to the lobby in back of the auditorium and asked someone how to get to the balcony. They showed him the stairs, and he took them two at a time. He quietly entered the balcony on the left and determined that there were two doors.

One door went directly into the sound booth. If he used that one, it would probably cause a gunfight during the service—not a pleasant thought. The other accessed a small room on his side of the sound room.

He very slowly, and quietly, moved to that door and opened it. Inside, he discovered a small podium and chairs, obviously set up for a class. But the most interesting thing was the fact that there was another door that allowed entry into the sound room.

*　　*　　*

Pastor Lancy announced in a loud voice, *"Please stand for the bridal entrance."*

Betty had selected Canon in D by Pachelbel to accompany her entrance. The organist and pianist played it beautifully, and they had added a cellist and violinist. It was sheer perfection. The flower girl proceeded Betty down the aisle scattering rose petals as she went. Betty, on the arm of her father, looked outstandingly beautiful in her off-shoulder, lace-sleeved tulle ballgown wedding dress with a huge flowing train. The train was held and guided by a second little girl, the twin of the flower girl.

Bob looked up the aisle as the entrance music started, and his heart almost stopped! His bride, Betty, was the most beautiful woman he had ever seen.

He thought, *That must be what every groom thinks.*

But then he thought, *No—she* is *the most beautiful woman I've ever seen!*

Betty was followed by her maid of honor and her bridesmaids. Everything was picture-perfect. They all reached the front of the church and lined up.

The pastor asked, *"Who gives this woman?"*

Betty's father said, *"My wife and I."*

And the marriage vows began.

*　　*　　*

The time was approaching. Tin Man raised his rifle and steadied it on the sound room windowsill. He sighted through the scope and placed the crosshairs on the left center of Bob Garver's back, right where the heart is located. Jack Lentor had the Sunday school classroom door cracked and was watching. He saw him raise the rifle.

*　　*　　*

Pastor Lancy had reached the reading of the vows:

"Do you, Betty, take this man, Robert Garver, as your lawfully wedded husband? To have and to hold from this day forward, for better, for worse, for richer, for poorer, in sickness and in health, to love and to cherish, till death do you part, according to God's holy ordinance?"

Betty said, *"I do."*

The pastor then asked Bob, *"Do you, Robert, take this woman, Betty Marcum, as your lawfully wedded wife? To have and to hold from this day forward, for better, for worse, for richer, for poorer, in sickness and in health, to love and to cherish, till death do you part, according to God's holy ordinance?"*

Bob was ready to make the final commitment, but suddenly a shot rang out from the balcony area. Someone with a rifle stood up in the sound booth and fired a shot toward the back of the sound booth. He then jumped out of the sound booth window and ran down the steps of the balcony. A second man appeared in the sound booth window, holding a pistol, and fired three shots at the man with the rifle. The man tripped, stumbled, and fell over the balcony railing twenty feet onto the center aisle of the auditorium facedown.

Confusion reigned, women screamed, and people started trying to get out of the auditorium. Pastor Lancy took control, speaking into the microphone, *"Calm down, folks! Everything is under control. Please take your seats for a moment. We have several policemen from Deer Park in the audience—they will take care of this!"* Although people were obviously still upset, they settled down.

Bob and Betty turned and ran down the aisle toward the fallen figure. On their way down the aisle, Betty had lifted up her wedding gown and pulled out a small concealed .38-caliber pistol. As they approached the body, the man rolled onto his side and pointed a 9 mm pistol at Bob. Betty shot the man in the arm he used for holding his pistol. It flew out of his hand, skittering down the church aisle. And for good measure, she shot him in the leg that he already limped on. He screamed and fell back unconscious.

By this time, Jack Lentor had left the sound booth, flown down the balcony stairs, and ran down the center aisle to the now disabled Tin Man.

He told Betty, *"Earlier, I saw someone with a rifle in the sound booth. I snuck in and caught him pointing it toward the front of the auditorium.*

I shot at him but missed in the excitement. It apparently scared him, and he took a quick shot at me and missed. Then he jumped out of the sound booth window. As he ran down the balcony stairs with the rifle, I shot at him three times, and apparently hit him at least once, causing him to fall over the balcony."

Betty gave Jack a hug, thanked him for saving their lives, and said, *"You need to spend more time at the gun practice range!"*

At that moment, two men appeared in the sound booth window. One still had duct tape hanging from his hands.

The other man said, *"I found Steve tied up and moaning here in the sound booth. What's going on? How come the wedding has stopped?"*

This caused the audience to break into laughter.

Bob turned to Betty and said, *"So that's where you keep your concealed weapon!"*

Betty said, *"And don't you forget it, buster! Now you answer Pastor Lancy's question. Do you take me for your lawfully wedded wife?"*

Loud enough for all to hear, Bob said, *"I do, I do, I do!"*

Pastor Lancy came up behind him and yelled, *"I now pronounce you man and wife."*

The crowd erupted in applause.

Being a Deer Park policewoman, on Betty's side of the auditorium, there were quite a few policemen and policewomen. They quickly organized, placed the Tin Man in handcuffs, performed first aid, read him his rights, and rushed him out to a waiting ambulance. He was taken to the hospital, accompanied by two policemen. Since Betty's shots had gone through cleanly, he was stitched up, and sent on his way to the calaboose! He would still be there when Bob and Betty returned from their honeymoon. A second ambulance was waiting for the sound booth man. Although he seemed to have recovered from the stun gun shock, they wanted him to be checked at the hospital.

The crowd was still a bit excited, so Betty went to the microphone and said, *"Would the wedding party please get back into your positions. I'm not about to let that nutball end our wedding on a sour note. And will the organist and pianist go to their instruments and play the exit march."*

The organist pulled out all the stops, the pianist lifted her piano top wide to allow all the sound out, and they began playing the "Wedding March" by Felix Mendelssohn at full volume.

Everyone had resumed their "pre-shot" positions, and the bride and groom smiled proudly as they marched down the aisle arm in arm. The crowd stood and began to applaud again, and everyone was giving the bride and groom happy smiles and high fives.

The pastor was heard to say, *"Well, that's the most interesting wedding I have ever conducted! I hope this doesn't catch on!"*

CHAPTER 31

THE RECEPTION

Betty found her mother and the wedding coordinator crying in the lobby. All of their hard work—for nothing.

Betty said, *"Mom, the objective was achieved. We're married! And you have to admit, the ceremony wasn't boring! Come on—other than delaying the reception for a few minutes, nothing has changed. You two have done a marvelous job, and we need to finish it the way you planned. How about making sure the reception can proceed."*

Linda Marker, the wedding coordinator, was the first to calm down.

She said, *"Betty's right! Nothing has changed! Let's get the reception started. Give us a few minutes before you send the people in."*

And off they went to put the toothpaste back in the tube.

Actually, they were the only two who had not recovered nicely. Most of the people were standing around in the lobby discussing the amazing events they had just witnessed. The original plan was to have an hour of hors d'oeuvres as a start to the reception. Betty's mother asked the invitees to move into the reception room, and soon they were busy talking and eating hors d'oeuvres. Betty's mother and Linda Marker circulated to make sure everything was being handled well. They were pleasantly surprised that the reception was proceeding as though nothing unusual had happened.

In fact, no one was having trouble making conversation—the "shotgun wedding" was the talk of the town. During this time, the wedding party was busy with the photographer snapping photos. Bob's parents were there, and Betty's father went back to the reception room to get his wife so the family photos could be taken. He caught Pastor Lancy and told him to have the deacons send him the bill for the damages from the gunfight.

The pastor remarked, *"Now that's a conversation I've never had with the deacon board!"*

The photographer was ready, obviously experienced, and had the right equipment, so it went very smoothly.

Bob asked him, *"Do you want us to bring the shooter back so you can get a photo of him falling from the balcony?"*

Betty gave him "that look!"

Toward the end of the hors d'oeuvres hour, the guests were seated for dinner, and the traditional wedding party entrances were started. First, the men in their tuxedos came in to a smattering of applause. Next, the maid of honor and her bridesmaids came in—much more applause. This was followed by the parents of the bride and groom being introduced. And finally, Betty and Bob, the new bride and groom made their grand entrance. The room erupted with standing applause for Mr. and Mrs. Garver!

The salads had already been placed on the tables. The small ensemble began to play softly some light dinner music. They were an excellent group. Betty hoped they would also be able to play some dance music later. The main entrée had been changed to filet mignon. Each table was systematically asked to move to the buffet line where the chefs had the steaks organized into rare, medium rare, medium, and well-done. They were hot and ready to go. The buffet included mashed potatoes and steamed vegetables as well as a number of other dishes. A separate carafe of gravy was supplied at each table for those wishing to increase their calorie count. The high moment of the meal came with dessert, which was Baked Alaska, served by the staff of waiters. No one went away hungry!

Ralph Swenson, in his role as best man, gave an outstanding toast.

He said, *"I've known Bob for over fifteen years. He used to be a salesman calling on me in New Jersey. He won his way into my heart by frequently taking me to lunch!"* (Laughter.) *"Since that time, he repented of his sins as a lying salesman and joined Massey Chemical Company— against my recommendation, of course."* (Laughter.) *"He has just finished the start-up of the largest olefins plant in the country. Of course, during his tenure there, the plant was burned down three times, and they had a major explosion!"* (Laughter.)

"But as they say, 'seriously, folks,' it has been a pleasure to know Bob, and to prove it, he is being moved into my group in head office Engineering as soon as he returns from his honeymoon—that is, if Betty isn't too hard on him. And regarding Betty—I haven't known her as long as Bob, but she is obviously an intelligent and beautiful woman. It is a mystery to me how Bob convinced her to marry him. As you all know, she is actually Lieutenant Betty Garver now—a Deer Park policewoman. It is my belief that it will take a policewoman to keep Bob in line—I certainly have never been able to do it!" (Laughter.) *"It was nice of her to demonstrate her prowess as a policewoman during the service we just witnessed!"* (Laughter.)

"Again, seriously, I ask you to raise your glasses to toast this wonderful new bride and groom. May they always be as happy as they are today. And at their fiftieth anniversary party, may they not have to shoot anyone!" (Laughter as the toast was drunk.)

Ralph then said, *"Now as the ensemble plays, let's congratulate Mr. and Mrs. Garver as they have their first dance as a married couple."* Bob and Betty started dancing and danced their way around the floor to the applause of the crowd. Ralph then asked Betty's parents to join them—then Bob's parents—and finally, he suggested everyone might want to join them. The music was wonderful, the people were obviously having a great time, and the reception was definitely back on track.

After things settled down a bit, the wedding cake was brought out. It was a huge six-tier vanilla cake. To maintain tradition, a photo was taken of Bob and Betty cutting the cake. Bob had seen some weddings where the groom pushed frosting into the bride's face as a joke. It never seemed funny to Bob, so they interlocked arms and fed each other a bite of the cake. The waiters then came up, finished cutting the cake, and gave it to the guests. Delicious.

The last event on the menu was the tossing of the bride's bouquet. This was organized by Betty's mother. The women gathered at one side of the dance floor, and Betty was on the other side facing away. On her mother's command, she threw the bouquet over her shoulder into the crowd of women. Who should catch it but Cindy Parker, Betty's roommate? It was sort of prophetic since Cindy had been dating the same guy for over a year, and he had just asked her to marry him. Everybody got a laugh out of that.

Closing the event, the dance floor was again opened for all couples. Bob and Betty took the opportunity to have a last dance before catching the limousine to their honeymoon suite at the airport. The flight to Hawaii was scheduled for 10:00 a.m. the next day. The crowd was given ten minutes to gather between the church exit and the limo so they could wish them well. In accordance with the latest ecology craziness, they threw birdseed instead of rice—theoretically because the rice might choke a bird. Bob asked Betty how many choked birds she had seen in her police days. Answer: None.

Bob said, *"Maybe for our next wedding, we can use cooked rice instead."*

Betty said, *"At our next wedding, I'll just settle for no gunshots!"*

Waving to the crowd, and giving each other a kiss for the camera, they got into the limo, and off they went.

C H A P T E R   3 2

CONFESSIONS AND CONVICTIONS

When Bob and Betty returned from their two-week honeymoon in Hawaii, another limousine was waiting at the airport to take them to Bob's apartment—which was where they intended to start married life. With Bob's blessing, Betty's mother had taken the task of making sure this bachelor apartment was fit for her daughter. The limo driver helped them carry their luggage up to the second-floor apartment. They thanked and tipped him—then entered their new home, where Betty's mother and father were waiting.

Wow! Betty's mother had outdone herself (with Betty's father paying the bills). Bob's old threadbare sofa and chairs had been replaced. The bare tile floor now had an area rug. Best of all, Bob's little TV set had been replaced by a forty-eight-inch ultra-definition smart TV. The apartment already had a fireplace, and Bob could just imagine sitting in front of a blazing fire, watching TV with his new bride.

The kitchenette area had a new table and chairs, and Betty's father had convinced the rental property owner to replace the stove, refrigerator, and dishwasher. Bob suspected that some major greenbacks had passed between them. In the bedroom, everything was new—king-sized bed, end tables, bureaus, and rug. They were both ecstatic over the changes Betty's mother had made.

Bob said, *"Mom and Dad—may I call you Mom and Dad?—this is over and beyond what either of us expected. You are miracle workers. Thank you very much. And especially, thank you for the wedding—it was fantastic!"*

Marsha answered for both of them, *"We enjoyed doing it. We just hope you two will be very happy here."*

They all hugged, and Betty's parents left for home, understanding that the new married couple would want to be alone after two weeks away.

The next Monday, Bob started his assignment at Massey head office in downtown Houston, where he was assigned as process control engineer on the reinstrumentation of a lubes hydrotreater unit in the Deer Park plant. The engineering contractor was also located in Houston, so he would be home every night.

Betty's job focus was on John Swisher and Marcus Stalinbeck (alias Tin Man). During their absence, the cases had moved from the police department to the district attorney's office, where one of their best assistant DAs had been assigned. Both of the accused had hired lawyers, and had been arraigned. An arraignment is a formal hearing where the accused is told what the charges are. He is also advised regarding his legal and constitutional rights. And finally, the judge asks how the person would like to plead. They both pleaded "innocent" to the charges. Bail is normally set at the arraignment, but since these cases involved conspiracy to commit murder, the judge did not allow bail. In John Swisher's case, he was known to have the funds needed to leave the country. In the Tin Man's case, the charges were just too serious, and the judge decided that there would be danger to the community if he was released on bail.

The next step would be for the cases to go before a grand jury, where the DA would try to convince the jury that there was enough evidence to proceed to trial. Betty would be advising during that step. However, she planned to get with each of the accused parties, with their lawyers present, and go over the massive evidence against them, hoping that they would buy into a lesser charge if they changed their plea to guilty. She also planned to play one against the other, offering a reduced sentence if they turned on the other person. Frankly, this was one of the "fun parts" of her job.

Since these crimes involved John Swisher hiring the Tin Man to commit arson, and later paying him to hire a second hit man to kill the witness, Bob Garver, the question came up: *"Who is guilty of what crime or crimes?"* The death of the Deer Park operator was obviously part of the arson charge. But the attempt to murder Bob Garver presented questions. First, the murder did not take place, so the charges would involve attempted murder. The hit woman who attempted to kill Bob at Shrimp Galore was dead—the law can't touch her. She has to answer to God.

The person who pulls the trigger (Tin Man) is guilty of attempted murder, which is serious because there obviously was premeditation in this case. If the murder had succeeded, typically the charge would have been first-degree murder, since killing someone for money is usually a death-penalty-eligible (or life without possibility of parole) offense. Since this was "attempted" murder, the penalty would obviously be less, but the premeditation would very likely cause a long sentence. The Tin Man would also be guilty of the lesser charge of conspiracy to commit murder, since he conspired with the buyer (Swisher) to arrange the killing of someone else.

What surprises some people is that, if the murder succeeds, the hiring party would also be guilty of first-degree murder. The legal argument for that is that the purchaser used the hit man as he would a gun to commit the murder. Again, since Swisher's hit man did not succeed, there would be no first-degree murder charge, but the sentence would reflect the serious nature of the attempt, and the fact that it was attempted several times. And just like the hit man, the hiring party is also guilty of conspiracy to commit murder for putting the plan into motion.

Betty asked Bob to come in and view a lineup including the Tin Man. She tried to select other men who resembled the Tin Man. Bob was the eyewitness who had seen him, first at Massey prior to the fire, secondly during his knife attack at his apartment, thirdly when he took the photos in the Houston Tunnel System, and finally when he shot at him on Smith Street. As soon as the lights were turned on in the lineup room (which was separated from the viewers by a one-way mirror), Bob immediately picked the Tin Man. His lawyer, who was present, tried to persuade Bob that he was really unsure—it had been dark, he was far away, events had been moving too fast, and other arguments.

But Bob said there was no way he was wrong—this was the Massey arsonist, the one who had attacked him with a knife at his apartment, and the one who shot at him on Smith Street. The lawyer finally gave up, recognizing this would be an uphill fight.

*　　*　　*

Since the lawyer was already present, the Tin Man was brought into an interrogation room. Betty laid out the evidence that would be used in his trial:

+ Bob Garver was a credible witness to all of his crimes.
+ They had warrant authorized recordings of phone calls between John Swisher and him.
+ They had warrant authorized phone records of calls between the hit woman and him.
+ They had bank records showing the transfer of $50,000 out of Swisher's offshore account, and the Tin Man's account receiving the same amount the next day.
+ They had warrant authorized recordings of his call to John Swisher arranging the additional payment of $5,000 for the expedited murder.
+ They had high-resolution videos and photos of John Swisher leaving $5,000 at the Waterwall.
+ Although these videos and photos could not identify the Tin Man because of his motorcycle clothes, they had located and searched his hotel room (with a warrant) and found the envelope with the $5,000. It had his and John Swisher's fingerprints on it.
+ They had found his hair at the Waterwall, and DNA evidence showed that he was there.
+ They found a boot print at the Waterwall, and it exactly matched the boot in his hotel room.
+ They found motorcycle clothing in his hotel room that matched the video and photos exactly.
+ They had an FBI agent's testimony that he actually saw the Tin Man attempt the murder at the wedding.
+ They also had a church pastor and about two hundred witnesses to the Tin Man's attempt at murder during the wedding service.

Most could pick him out of a lineup since they got a great look at him when he was faceup on the church floor.

Betty said that they had much more, but it could wait for the trial. The lawyer said he wanted to talk with his client alone. That was arranged, and when they came back, he asked what kind of a deal they would offer.

Betty said, *"I can't make deals, but if your client changes his plea to guilty, I will ask the DA to reduce the sentence from 'life without parole' to 'life with the possibility of parole.' In addition, I think if your client will turn State's evidence against John Swisher, the DA may reduce that to a twenty-five-year sentence. He would only be fifty-five when he gets out."*

The lawyer looked at the Tin Man, he nodded, and the lawyer asked Betty to check it out with the DA. It only took a phone call to get the deal authorized.

*　　*　　*

It was now John Swisher's turn. Betty was really going to enjoy this. Swisher's attitude when she interviewed him was downright nasty. He treated her like she was his servant. With his lawyer present, Betty listed the evidence against Swisher, saving the best until last:

+ They had warrant authorized recordings of several phone calls between Swisher and Marcus Stalinbeck (alias the Tin Man).
+ They had a warrant authorized phone records of calls between the Tin Man and the Hit Woman.
+ They had bank records showing the transfer of $50,000 out of Swisher's offshore account, and the Tin Man's account receiving the same amount the next day.
+ They had warrant authorized recordings of Swisher and the Tin Man negotiating the additional $5,000 payment to speed up the killing of the witness.
+ They had bank records showing the transfer of $5,000 cash from Swisher's Houston account.
+ They showed Swisher and his lawyer high-resolution videos and photos of John Swisher leaving $5,000 at the Waterwall, and it being picked up by the Tin Man on his motorcycle.

Swisher's lawyer said, *"You can't possibly tell who the person on the motorcycle is. John may have been passing money to someone he owed."*

Betty laughed. *"Yeah, right. I always make my Visa payments that way."*

+ They described Swisher's high-speed attempt to escape the police, endangering many people on the Southwest Freeway.
+ They noted the $5,000 payment was found in the Tin Man's hotel room. It had Swisher's fingerprints on the money and the envelope. (So much for the Visa payment.)

Then Betty said, *"But just wait—I've been saving the best for last."*

+ Marcus Stalinbeck (the Tin Man) has agreed to turn State's evidence and testify against you, providing all the details of the conspiracy.

Betty concluded, *"It's all over, Swisher, you're as guilty as sin."*

The lawyer said, *"Can we talk a deal here?"*

Betty said, *"No way—your client will be convicted easily of conspiracy to commit murder. If you persist in the innocent plea, you can expect the jury to give him the longest sentence possible, since the act was obviously premeditated, extended over several weeks with opportunities to reverse it. And he shows no sign of even knowing it was wrong. The evidence is truly overwhelming. You may wish to change your plea to guilty and hope for a lenient judge. This interview is over."*

Betty had to control herself to keep from skipping down the hall yelling, "Yea! We did it!"

Betty got Bob out of the interrogation room viewing area and asked him what he thought of the interviews with the Tin Man and John Swisher.

Bob said, *"Betty, it was like you were a ferocious cat, and they were mice in a trap! You were great! So, then it is almost over. When are the trials?"*

Betty said, *"The DA wants these cases to proceed at warp speed, and he has some clout regarding the judges' case assignments, so I suspect they will be held within thirty days. Maybe you can stop carrying your weapon after that."*

Bob replied, *"No way, our wedding showed me where you carry yours, and I need to defend myself!"*

They both laughed, but were secretly relieved that it was close to over.

It took longer than Betty predicted, but eventually the judge took the Tin Man's guilty plea and the DA's deal into account, sending him to prison for twenty-five years with the possibility of parole. John Swisher's trial was a few weeks later. The lawyer had advised Swisher to stay with his innocent plea, which was a big mistake. The Tin Man testified at the trial, revealing all the nitty-gritty details of the crimes. The evidence was overwhelming, and the high-resolution videos of the dead drop at the Waterwall clinched it in the jurors' minds. Swisher made the mistake of testifying in his own behalf—during which he showed his "superior" attitude and no repentance. The prosecutor tore him apart! The jury was only out for fifteen minutes, returning a guilty verdict and recommending that the judge give him the most severe sentence possible. He was sentenced to fifty years in prison with no opportunity for parole until after forty years. Swisher would be eighty-five years old before he had any chance of leaving prison. As they say, *"Good riddance to bad rubbish."*

EPILOGUE

Now we move fifty years into the future.

Bob and Betty are celebrating their fiftieth wedding anniversary. Their daughter, Cindy (named after Betty's roommate), has organized a party at the Faith Community Church, where they are still attending (Bob is now an elder, both in age and in office). In attendance are their five children: one girl (Cindy), two boys, and a set of boy/girl twins. In addition, there are seven grandchildren ranging from teenagers to kids in diapers. Their parents are doing their best to keep the kids from tearing the church apart. Cindy has arranged multiple decorations indicating fifty years of marriage, including a large number of #50 balloons. At the end of the party, each of the kids will take a few balloons, and they will all release them into the sky at once—symbolic that there is more to come.

Cindy reads a nice tribute to her parents. It brings tears to her eyes, as well as to others' in attendance; and Betty gives her a big hug. Bob and Betty's many friends are there. Other than a few Massey and Deer Park Police retirees, most of them have become friends in this church over the years. Bob and Betty have both been very active members. Bob has retired from Massey Chemical after thirty-two years of service and has used part of their savings to purchase a weekend place on Lake Livingston, about one and a half hours from Deer Park. Their grandkids think the boating, waterskiing, jet skiing, and swimming make it the best place on earth. Betty has retired from the police force as a captain, and they are enjoying their uninterrupted time together. They are still as much in love as they were fifty years ago.

Both Bob's and Betty's parents have passed away about ten years ago. Betty's brother, Bill Marcum, has also retired and visits them infrequently. Betty's roommate, Cindy Parker, passed away about ten years after their marriage. She had "inherited" Betty's dog, Robber, and her cat, Bandit, following the wedding, since Bob's apartment would not allow pets. By the time they had purchased a house, the pets were comfortable with Cindy, and she outlived them both.

Bob's old boss and best man, Ralph Swenson, is still alive, but due to the aging process, he is in a nursing home. Bob visits him once in a while to reminisce over old times. Frank Baron, Bob's first boss at the Deer Park start-up team, has passed away. Most of Bob's Massey Chemical friends have retired, but the ones who live in the Houston area meet once a quarter for lunch just to keep in touch. Over the years, Bob Esterbrook, Fred Conway, Jack Fishbane, Harold Neymeir, John Cross, Doc Harpy, "Long John" Whippet, and several others have been added to the group. Mack "the Hack" Turner, and his cohort, Sam Peck, are young enough that they are still "hacking away" for the Deer Park Police Department on their computer equipment.

Jack Lentor, the FBI agent, is now working in Washington, DC, running their counterespionage units. He calls about once a year to see how Bob and Betty are doing. Bob jokes with him that he is just waiting for Bob to die so he can marry Betty. Jack's wife has died, and he plans to retire from the FBI within a couple of years. Randy Simcon, the FBI camera expert, has retired.

John Swisher, who conspired to kill Bob, served his forty years in prison (before the possibility of parole). Bob did a bit of investigating and found out that John had accepted Christ in prison as a result of the efforts of Prison Fellowship. Bob visited him and found that his attitude had completely changed. He expressed sorrow for what he had done and asked Bob to forgive him. That was no problem for Bob, since Christ had forgiven Bob for all of his sins. Bob and several other Christians appeared at John's parole hearing, testifying on his behalf, and he presently is on parole, living in Dallas. His conversion was apparently real, his life has completely turned around, and he serves in a large Dallas church.

The Tin Man, Marcus Stalinbeck, has served his twenty-five-year sentence and has been released from prison. His experience with the evidence produced by the high-definition photos and videos caused him to take courses in prison. He now runs a successful home surveillance business, is married, and lives happily in Fort Worth, Texas.

I guess it is true, *"all's well that ends well."*

Lightning Source UK Ltd.
Milton Keynes UK
UKHW010037280721
387881UK00007B/422/J